Ed Drops In

We were still sitting at the kitchen table when there was a noise on the roof. We looked at one another. There it was again. It sounded like footsteps.

Then we heard it—a bellow and a bone-chilling "Yeeoww!" There was a thump and then a thudding sound, like something tumbling from the chimney to the gutter.

Then I saw it.

The face of a big gorilla had appeared upside down in the kitchen window. It was there for only an instant, and then it dropped out of sight.

I looked into Coach Donovan's eyes, composed myself, and said, "Hibby hibby gogo." I'd wanted to say "Let's hide."

Before I could try again, the kitchen door opened . . .

. . . and it walked in.

BRIAN DALY

A MINSTREL® BOOK

PUBLISHED BY POCKET BOOKS

New York   London   Toronto   Sydney   Tokyo   Singapore

This book is a work of fiction. Names, characters, places, and incidents are products of the author's imagination or are used fictitiously. Any resemblance to actual events or locales or persons, living or dead, is entirely coincidental.

A MINSTREL PAPERBACK *Original*

 A Minstrel Book published by
POCKET BOOKS, a division of Simon & Schuster Inc.
1230 Avenue of the Americas, New York, NY 10020

ISBN: 0-671-87111-0

First Minstrel Books printing December 1994

10 9 8 7 6 5 4 3 2

A MINSTREL BOOK and colophon are registered trademarks of Simon & Schuster Inc.

Cover art by Dan Burr

Printed in the U.S.A.

For Laurel

Preface

———●———

My name is Picasso Dewlap. I'm a seventh grader at Spruce Island Middle School in Maine. We moved here to the island from Chicago last year when I was in sixth because my father got a job with the Bumstock Lawn Ornament Company. He designs ceramic lawn ornaments. They're the little statues—usually stuff like pink flamingos and elves and birdbaths—that people put out on their lawns for decoration.

We moved in early November. That's when I started keeping a journal. I thought I'd have lots of exciting adventures living on an island, and I wanted to write them all down and make a book out of them—and then sell the story to Hollywood, and I'd star in the movie and do my own stunts and everything and be a millionaire by the time I started high school.

But life on Spruce Island was boring. I didn't catch a great white shark or ride on the back of a whale or even rescue a drowning fisherman. I just went to school and came home and wondered when I was going to make some friends and have some fun.

I thought I could make friends if I was on the basketball team, so I tried out. And guess what—I made it! (Even though I was lousy.) Only a couple of guys got cut from the team, and they were even worse than I was—believe it or not.

Anyway, I've written this preface to let you know what went on before my book starts. Believe me, you wouldn't want to read the entries in my journal before I went out for the basketball team. Even some of them after I made the team could put you to sleep.

The good stuff started on December 19, so that's the beginning of this book.

I've done my best to write an accurate account of the story—you know, what people looked like and who said what and everything—so whoever reads this book can get a clear idea of what went on. I didn't write the story for myself. I didn't need to. I could never forget what happened if I live to be a hundred.

December 19

Tonight was the first game of our basketball season—and the first real game of my life.

I felt like a pro during the pregame stuff. We have these great-looking warm-ups; they're green and white with the name of the school on the front and "Lawn Ornaments" on the back. (I know it's a dopey name for a team, but the Bumstock Lawn Ornament Company provides all our equipment. So what are we supposed to do?)

Anyway, the pep band was playing and the bleachers were filling up fast and it felt so good to be on a real basketball team getting ready to play a real game with officials and cheerleaders and fans and everything that I missed all my practice layups. I kept bouncing on the balls of my feet and swinging my arms while I waited for my turn in the layup line. I just couldn't keep still.

Roland LeMay, our captain, said, "Hey, Dewlap, got to go to the bathroom?" He has a nasty way of saying something and then turning away before you can say something back—not that I wanted to. I don't want to step on any toes when I'm so new on the island.

But I guess I did have ants in my pants, because even when I sat down at the end of the bench when the game started, I kept on squirming. It was bad enough trying to keep calm while I watched the game—I couldn't imagine what it would be like if I actually had to play.

Well, I found out soon enough.

I was just sitting there on the bench, yelling my head off for the Lawn Ornaments, when a shadow fell over me. I looked up—way up—at Mr. Donovan, our coach. He's tall and wide and blocks plenty of light. "Picasso," he said, "get in there for Roland."

I don't know if I said anything to Mr. Donovan or how I got out of my warm-ups or even if I checked in at the scorer's table. The next thing I remember is standing on the court feeling very light, as if I could fly. I remember the air feeling cool when it touched my bare arms and legs. Everything seemed extra real—too bright, too loud, too fast.

I don't know what I did. I suppose I played. What I remember most is sitting back down on the bench a few minutes later and thinking, "There, I've done it. I've played basketball."

I got in the game for a few minutes during the second and third quarters, too, and that good feeling stayed with me. Then Mr. Donovan put me in again at the end of the game with two minutes left. I wish I could have stayed on the bench—or at home. The pressure was unbelievable because we were only one point behind the Edmund S. Muskie Middle School Senators, and the stands were full of basketball-crazy islanders. (Ever since Spruce Island High School closed and the island kids started going to the big regional high school on the mainland, the middle school basketball team has been *the* center of attention out here.)

I tried to concentrate on playing defense. I didn't want to *touch* the ball on offense. Nobody was going to blame me for missing a shot and losing the game.

Well, I guess everybody was tense, because neither team scored for a long time. Then, with five seconds left in the game, I found the ball in my hands. Once again, I don't know how it got there, but there it was, and I had to do something with it fast—but what?

A whole bunch of thoughts started running through my brain, one right after another. I must have used up a day's worth of thinking in a couple of seconds. "Take the shot," said my brain (*to* my brain, I guess). "You're only twelve feet from the basket. If you make it you'll be the hero and get your picture in the *Rocky Coast Blabber.* Go ahead." But then, one microzillionth of a second later, my brain said, "If you miss it, everybody on Spruce Island will hate you forever and you'll grow old alone and when you die nobody

5

will go to your funeral—they'll only stick a cheap marker up over your grave and it'll say, 'He missed.' "

I decided to pass.

The problem with that idea was I didn't have anybody to pass to. All our guys were rushing to the basket to get in position for the rebound in case I missed. As usual, Dexter Madison, a rugged, quiet kid who's our best rebounder, was close to the hoop, and even Roland LeMay, who usually just shoots, was looking for the rebound.

I probably should have put up the shot right then, but my stupid brain kept working and said, "Losing the game for your team is no way to make friends." I had to agree.

Just then two of the Muskie guys came running at me—and that's when I heard everybody in the gym yell, "Shoot!" So I shot—and missed.

But I got fouled!

With no time left on the clock, I went to the foul line for two shots. If I made one, we'd go into overtime. If I made two, we'd win and I'd become an instant immortal.

I put up my first shot. It rolled around the rim and out. The islanders groaned.

When I got the ball for my second shot, I let out a deep breath and bent my knees, but the ball felt funny in my hands, so I didn't shoot it. I dribbled it three times instead. Then I stared at the basket. It looked small, and the ball felt way too big, but I couldn't postpone taking the shot any longer. I shot.

I missed everything—except the floor.

Boy, it's funny how quiet a gym can get. The islanders put on their coats and hats and stared at me as they filed out.

Maybe I'm just touchy, but I think it's a little weird for adults to take middle school basketball so seriously.

Roland came up to me holding the ball in his hands. He was really mad. "You're an idiot, Dewlap, you doofus!" he said. "You blew it! We could've won, but you blew it!" He kept slamming the ball into the palm of his hand while he yelled at me. By the way, he spits like a fountain when he yells. What a jerk. And he thinks he's so great because he has this stupid little mustache.

I was the last one to walk into the locker room. I went straight to my locker and put a sweater and pants on right over my uniform. I wanted to get out of there fast—before anybody could figure out how to drown me in the showers and make it look like suicide.

Mr. Donovan came in and started to make a speech. I didn't look at him. Why would I want to look at him while he was banishing me to Siberia? I already knew what he looked like: short black hair, black beard, green eyes, big nose. . . .

"Lawn Ornaments," he said, "we had a chance to pull this one out tonight, but we came up a little short." I was preparing to hear him announce my sentence, but he only said, "Next time we'll get 'em."

7

That was it—nothing about what a goober I was or anything. I couldn't believe it. I was still a free man!

When I went outside, Victor and Elizabeth (my parents) were horsing around in the snow on the school lawn, grabbing each other's knit caps—their caps are extra long and hang down to their knees—and chasing each other around in circles like puppies.

(By the way, I call them Victor and Elizabeth instead of Dad and Mom because they want me to, not because I want to.)

Victor said, "There he is! There's Spruce Island's answer to Willie Mays!"

I told him Willie Mays used to be a baseball player.

He said, "Well, I bet he couldn't play basketball as well as you."

Then they both hugged me at the same time, smothering me between their coats. They're like that.

Elizabeth said, "Let's go to Rodney's and celebrate!"

"I don't feel much like celebrating," I said. "I lost the game for us."

"Nonsense," said Elizabeth. "It wasn't your fault. The other team simply scored too many points. I'd blame them."

"So would I," said Victor. "Now let's go to Rodney's."

My parents don't know much about basketball.

They took off for Rodney's ahead of me. I was glad they were ahead of me because they were—skipping.

Victor and Elizabeth were pretty old when they got married. They're about twenty years older than my teammates' parents, but they don't act it.

I followed them down Main Street. It's a pretty strange-looking village. Orange ceramic basketballs are on top of all the lampposts. Most of the houses have a ceramic cat attached to an outside wall. When we moved here six weeks ago, I thought it was funny to see ceramic duck families on every front lawn, but now I'm used to it—although it's getting harder to see them with a foot of snow on the ground.

The source of all these ceramic decorations is, of course, the Bumstock Lawn Ornament Company, Spruce Island's major employer. They make the lawn ornaments in an impressive old-fashioned ivy-covered factory. As we got near it, I noticed that the giant gold Bumstock sign on the roof looked nice with snow on top of the letters.

The night crew was working inside, putting ceramic molds into the huge ovens (they're called *kilns*) that bake the ornaments. The kilns are so hot that they keep the ground around them at the rear of the factory free of snow and ice and frost even in the coldest weather.

I thought I saw something big and dark moving across the bare ground by the kilns—something really big—but I didn't get a chance to investigate because Victor and Elizabeth were calling me. They wanted me to slide down the icy hill to Rodney's with them.

They're pretty goofy for parents, which can be embarrassing, but they can be a lot of fun, too—especially when nobody's around to see.

They sat down and slid on their rear ends. I stood up and made believe I was skiing.

Rodney's Café is located on the waterfront, next to the public landing, and it's the only restaurant on the island. Barbara Seabury has owned the place since Rodney retired. I guess the people who live here like their traditions, because now they all call Barbara "Rodney."

One tradition *I* like is the free hamburgers she gives to Lawn Ornaments after games.

We sat in a booth near the front door. While we waited to place our orders, Victor and Elizabeth looked into each other's eyes, and I listened to a conversation that was going on near the cash register. Actually it wasn't a conversation; it was a speech, and it was being delivered by Ludlow Bumstock, the owner and president of the Bumstock Lawn Ornament Company. He's a rich old bachelor who's nutty about lawn ornaments and Spruce Island Middle School basketball. A few people on the island make a living fishing and lobstering and clamming, and some people work on the mainland, but most of the islanders work for the Bumstock Lawn Ornament Company, so when Mr. Bumstock feels like making a speech, people listen. This is what he said.

"Spruce Island is famous for two things: lawn ornaments and basketball. Bumstock lawn ornaments are still the finest made in America, but, by Godfrey, our glorious tradition of basketball excellence started by ol' Doc Thompson and passed along to Sonny Doc Thompson is on its way out. And who do we have to thank for that? Donovan, that's who! This big overgrown goon of a coach comes here from away—now that Sonny Doc has turned his back on us and retired to Florida—and thinks he can do things his own way, thinks he can let every boy on the team play in every game and still have a winning season. Well, let me tell you—it can't be done!"

At this point in the speech, I was seeing how far down I could slump in my seat without falling on the floor. It's not much fun listening to the most powerful person in your community go on and on about how the subs blew the game, especially when you're the worst of the subs and the one—*the one*—who lost the game.

Mr. Bumstock continued. "This could be the first year that Spruce Island fails to make the tournament. Think of it!"

The islanders lowered their heads and studied the linoleum floor, trying to picture what life would be like without the Lawn Ornaments in the Down East League tournament.

Just then the front door of Rodney's flew open and Dexter Madison ran in and hollered, "I seen a bear rowing a dinghy!"

That made me sit up straight.

It got everybody's attention, even Victor and Eliza-

beth's. Nobody had ever seen Dexter so excited before. Rodney leaned over the counter and said,
"Maybe it was a man rowing a dinghy. Sometimes our
eyes play tricks on us, dear, and at night, well—"

"That was no man," said Dexter, "it was a bear. *I
seen a giant bear out there rowing a dinghy.*"

December 20

●────────────────────────●

When I was in bed last night, I thought a lot about what I saw, or thought I saw, behind the factory and what Dexter said he had seen out in the dinghy, and I wondered if there was a connection. I took him seriously because he's not the kind of guy who goes around making up wild stories. Some of the people at Rodney's, though, laughed at him after he left, and today at school kids whispered about him behind his back.

I felt sorry for him.

At the end of the school day we had practice, and it was a lousy one. Mr. Donovan walked us through our plays and told us how important it is to stick with the play and not go off on our own. He said if we worked together, we could win. He made sense, and all of us nodded.

Then we scrimmaged and forgot everything he told

us. It was every man for himself. We all shot whether we were open or not, and nobody stuck to his job on defense. Something was stinking up the gym—maybe it was the mudflats, but I think it was us.

Downstairs in the locker room after practice, Roland kept bugging me about missing those stupid foul shots last night. He kept it up until Dexter went into the showers. Then he said, "I always knew Dexter was stupid, but I never thought he was crazy until last night. Can you believe it? A giant bear rowing a dinghy? No wonder he keeps his mouth shut all the time. When he opens it, he sounds mental!"

Dexter couldn't hear him over the sound of the piped-in music in our showers. (We get instrumental versions of current hits so we can sing along.) If he had heard Roland, he probably would have pounded him. Dexter digs clams, and all that hard work has built him up.

I didn't want to hear any more from Roland, so I put on my earphones and turned up the music. (Every Lawn Ornament has a stereo FM radio–compact disc player with earphones for private listening, plus an extra-wide locker with a full-length mirror inside the door, a canvas director's chair, and a hair dryer.)

You've probably concluded that our locker room is pretty swanky. You're right. It's much nicer than the rest of the school, except the gym, of course. That's nice, too. Mr. Bumstock wants us Lawn Ornaments to have the best of everything.

As I left the locker room, I heard Dexter call out,

"Dewlap! Come here!" I made believe I didn't hear him. I didn't need another guy to tell me I'd lost the game for us.

There were purple shadows on the snow when I got outside. You know, even though there's snow on the ground, it's not as cold here as I thought it would be. Maine winters get pretty cold way up north in the deep woods, but most of the time here on the coast they're not bad at all. Maybe you'd think the ocean would chill everything, but it really keeps the temperature sort of moderate—not too cold in the winter and not too hot in the summer.

Anyway, it was nice to be out in the fresh air smelling the pines and the salty ocean instead of sweaty kids.

When I was walking home along Main Street and getting close to the Bumstock Lawn Ornament Company, I decided to go out by the kilns and look for signs that a giant bear had been there.

I walked around to the back of the factory. Things looked the same as usual. As I got nearer to the kilns, the snow cover grew thinner, and before long I was walking on grass. I didn't see any sign of the bear— or (gulp) the bear itself—but then something caught my eye. On some muddy ground right next to the kilns I saw a depression that could have been the pawprint of a bear, but actually it looked more like a human *footprint—a big one.*

December 23

———●———

A crib-stone bridge connects Spruce Island to the mainland. It's made of slabs of Maine granite put together checkerboard-style with spaces to allow the tides to flow through. A zillion trucks full of Bumstock lawn ornaments have rolled over it, carrying garden sundials and ceramic gnomes to all of America. Tonight it supported our team bus and a long line of cars and pickup trucks making the trip to Rockweed Harbor for a game against the Fightin' Clams.

I sat by myself and stared out at the moonlight on the Atlantic. I wondered if I ought to tell Dexter about the footprint I'd found near the kilns. I had almost told him a couple of times today, but I don't know the guy very well, and I've been afraid he'd think I was teasing him and pulverize me. Apparently he'd forgotten that he was going to speak to me about losing the game, and I didn't want to remind him.

16

While I was thinking, someone tapped me on the shoulder. I turned around. It was Roland LeMay. He leaned close to me and showed me a section of an orange. He pointed to it and said, "If you lose this game for us, this is your head." Then he squeezed the orange section and let the juice drip on my jacket. "Get it? I'll murderlize you."

Or course I got it. This audiovisual threat wasn't anything new—but it was effective.

The Spruce Island fans followed us into the parking lot at Rockweed Harbor Middle School. We stayed on the bus until they had gathered in two lines that stretched from the bus to the door of the school gym—sort of a human hallway. Then Mr. Donovan stood up and banged his head on the ceiling of the bus. "Let's go, Lawn Ornaments!" he said as he rubbed the bump on his head.

We all walked through the human hallway as the pep band played and the islanders slapped our hands. I heard two fans chant, "Picasso Dewlap's number one! He's our one and only son!"

Victor and Elizabeth.

When I passed in front of them, they showered me with confetti. Here I am trying to fit in with the kids in school, and my parents throw confetti at me. Mr. Inconspicuous, that's me.

I have to give Victor and Elizabeth credit, though. As soon as they had thrown all their confetti, they cleaned it right up with portable vacuum cleaners.

We used the girls' locker room because the Fightin'

17

Clams were in the boys' locker room. I don't know what I thought I'd see in there—maybe frilly pink fluffy dollhouse-type stuff or something, I don't know—but I never thought it would look as dreary as it did. There were wooden benches, gray lockers, and a wire barricade from the floor to the ceiling to separate the locker area from the shower area. Little wire cages covered the bare lightbulbs. It looked like a women's prison.

I was glad to get out of there and start the game.

We played a 2–3 zone defense. I was one of the two guards out front. I got in a few times in the first half and did okay. At least I didn't make any big mistakes.

Roland was having a great game. He doesn't do much on defense and he isn't much of a rebounder (he's not much of a human being, either, in my opinion), but the guy can shoot, and he was hot tonight.

Mr. Donovan let all twelve of us play, and his strategy seemed to work; the half ended with the score tied.

We all felt pretty good shooting around before the start of the second half. Roland was showing off for the cheerleaders, bombing from way outside and trying to look casual. He thinks he's so great. I overheard him say, "I hear Dexter's going to learn how to water-ski this summer if he can get his bear to row fast enough."

Dexter's ears turned red, and he was breathing like a bull.

We played even better in the second half and built up a seven-point lead early in the fourth quarter. Roland was still shooting well, and Dexter was grabbing lots of rebounds. He was still mad at Roland, but I guess he was using his anger to help him be aggressive under the boards (not that he needs much help).

Owen O'Malley (we call him O.) was playing with a lot of confidence and hitting from outside. It's a wonder he can see the basket; he has long, stringy, curly hair like Larry of the Three Stooges must have had before he went bald, and it's always hanging down in his eyes. He's supposed to be our center—he's the tallest guy on the team—but he hardly ever plays under the basket because he doesn't like the contact. He's awfully skinny.

With about four minutes left in the game, the Fightin' Clams started catching up. Roland was hogging the ball and taking all the shots. Then whenever he missed, he'd blame his teammates. What a jerk.

Mr. Donovan took him out.

O. got this crazy look in his eyes and said, "Don't worry, Mr. Donovan. When I get the ball in the O Zone, I'm unstoppable." He considers the O Zone to be anything inside twenty feet, and when he's in and Roland's out, he bombs away.

Well, O. sent plenty of bombs through the O Zone, but all of them were duds. Mr. Donovan called time and benched him.

It occurred to me that I might have to go in for the

end of the game. I got a mental picture of us losing and Roland squeezing my head until everything gushed out.

"Picasso."

"Huh?" I said, sounding really intelligent.

"Go check in and get in there." It was Mr. Donovan talking to me.

I stayed put. Mr. Donovan acted puzzled. I still didn't budge.

"What's the matter?" he asked.

I said, "I'm not feeling so good," which was the truth. I'd worked myself into an upset stomach. "I think I have the flu—the Canadian flu. It's the kind of flu that puts you in the hospital if you run around and get sweaty. I think I'd better stay on the bench just to play it safe." And that was the truth, too. If we were going to lose, it was safer for me to be on the bench than on the court.

Roland stood up and said, "Put me in."

Mr. Donovan said, "Sit down." Roland sat down and pouted.

Somebody else went in, and we lost, but I got to stay on the bench and keep my head in its traditional shape with all its contents intact.

In the locker room after the game, Roland was muttering under his breath. "Donovan doesn't know how to coach. He doesn't know anything. He's just a big stupid hairy gorilla."

That's when Mr. Bumstock walked in. He said, "Where's Donovan?"

"Here I am," said Mr. Donovan. He had been changing his shirt and came out bare-chested. He's hairy all over, even on his back. "Pretty good game, huh? I think the boys are coming along well."

"Yes, they are. But unfortunately, you are not. You don't know how to coach."

"Wait just a minute," said Mr. Donovan, and the Lawn Ornaments looked shocked. I guess they'd never heard anybody talk back to Mr. Bumstock before. "I appreciate your interest in the team, and I'm grateful for all the financial support you've given us, but, hey, leave the coaching to me. This is my team."

"No, it is not," said Mr. Bumstock. "This is Spruce Island's team. It's been our *only* team ever since the state closed our beloved Spruce Island High. Maybe you don't know it, young fella, but I played for Spruce Island High under ol' Doc Thompson, and we won the state championship in Class D. Island boys. State *champeens*. In the old days it meant something to play for Spruce Island."

"It still does. And it means something to me to coach here."

"Oh, it does? Well, then, you'd better start winning." Mr. Bumstock poked his finger into Mr. Donovan's hairy chest. "The Lawn Ornaments won under ol' Doc Thompson and they won under Sonny Doc Thompson. Now you're here and they're losing. Isn't that grand?" He was really getting mad. "Let me tell

21

you something, Mr. Man. If the Lawn Ornaments don't make it into the tournament, you're through. Understand me, Donovan? Through!''

Then Mr. Bumstock walked to the door, turned around, and, looking at Mr. Donovan through squinty eyes, said, "Merry Christmas."

December 24

●────────────●

*A*fter supper, Victor and Elizabeth went down to
the cellar to make their annual "Christmas Creation."
They express their holiday joy by making art. I think
it's a great idea. It's always fun to wake up Christmas
morning to see what they've made.

They didn't want me to peek, so Elizabeth sent me
to Mr. Donovan's with one of her special Yuletide
pies. I have a feeling that everybody who receives one
is glad Christmas comes just once a year.

I looked up at the stars as I walked along the road
to Mr. Donovan's house. He and his wife live on the
edge of the woods, far from any other houses.

I knocked on the kitchen door, and Mr. Donovan
opened it. He looks big at school, but in a house he's
enormous. Wow. I could hear somebody sniffling on
the other side of the door, and I figured it was Mrs.
Donovan. They don't have any kids, so who else could
it have been?

"My mother sent me over with this," I said. "It's a pickle pie."

I handed it over and started to leave before he could invite me in—it's pretty weird to see a teacher outside of school living just like a regular person—but Mrs. Donovan stuck her head out from behind the door and said, "Come in, come in. Please."

They took me into the living room, and Mrs. Donovan turned on the Christmas tree lights and the radio. She seemed pretty happy to have company, even if it was only me. Then she cut into the pickle pie and offered me some, but I knew better than to take a piece. I had some Christmas cookies and a cup of cocoa instead.

The Donovans were really nice, and I got used to visiting with them in no time at all. Everything was going along great, we were talking and everything, and then I asked a question that I would regret in a minute and a half: "How do you like living on the island?"

She said, "Well, the scenery's nice." That was all. I took a look at the expression on her face, decided it wasn't happy, and thought I'd better drop the interrogation.

But she went on.

"The problem is I can't talk to the scenery."

Mr. Donovan said, "Well, you can, but it can't talk back."

Mrs. Donovan ignored him and said, "Nobody drops by to visit, but the strange thing is I feel somebody watching me during the day while you're all in school. I know that's ridiculous; we don't have any neighbors, and there are never any hunters out in the woods, but just the same, I get the feeling that there are eyes out there looking at me."

I was getting the creeps.

Mr. Donovan tried to cheer her up. He said, "Maybe it's Dexter Madison's giant bear," and he laughed.

"What do you mean?" asked Mrs. Donovan.

"Haven't you heard about the giant bear rowing the dinghy?"

"No. None of the hundreds of friends I've made out here on the island have mentioned it to me."

I know sarcasm when I hear it. That's when I regretted bringing up the subject.

Nobody said anything. While I debated saying something about the footprint I had found out behind the kilns, Mrs. Donovan put her first forkful of pickle pie into her mouth. I kept quiet and hoped she wouldn't throw up.

Instead, she started to cry.

"I'm sorry about the pie," I said. "You don't have to eat it."

"It's not the pie, it's the song." "Rockin' Around the Christmas Tree" was playing on the radio. "My sisters and I used to play that record and do the jitterbug in the kitchen every Christmas." Her bottom lip was trembling. "This is the first Christmas I've been away from them."

Mr. Donovan put his arm around her. I felt pretty

embarrassed, and I was wondering if I could sneak out without them noticing, but Mr. Donovan said to me, "Sometimes it gets lonely being in a new place."

I said, "I know."

For a minute, seeing Mrs. Donovan looking so sad made me feel kind of grown up, because she was having a tougher time getting used to living on the island than I was, but then I felt like a baby because all that crying was making *me* feel like crying.

I guess Mr. Donovan remembered that I'm new here, too, and knew how I was feeling, because he changed the subject. "Hey, what do you want for Christmas, Picasso? What's ol' Santa going to bring you this year?"

I felt like saying "a friend," but all I said was "I don't know." (Sometimes I can be a scintillating conversationalist.)

Mr. Donovan said, "I know what I want. I'd like a really tall kid who can run and jump and shoot and play defense. Maybe then we'd make it into the tournament and Bumstock would get off my back."

I had had my fill of adult problems for one night, so I drained my cup of cocoa and stood up.

"Got to go so soon?" said Mr. Donovan.

"Yup." (How do I think up these witty things to say?)

As I put on my jacket, Mrs. Donovan said, "Can you come back tomorrow afternoon?"

"I don't know."

"Please?"

"Okay."

December 25

―――――――――●―――――――――

We always have a great-looking Christmas tree. Victor has made lots of beautiful ceramic tree ornaments for us over the years, mostly what he calls non-representational stuff—that is, they don't look like anything in particular, and Elizabeth always finds colorful stuff to put on the tree; she puts scraps of cloth together with junk that other people would call . . . well, junk, and makes the tree look like a treasure in a castle or something.

We sat on the floor and exchanged presents. I gave Victor and Elizabeth art supplies—as usual.

As I unwrapped my first present, I had a feeling it was a sweater (because Elizabeth *always* knits a sweater for me), and it was. It was a replica of the Spruce Island Middle School varsity letter jacket.

"What do you think?" asked Elizabeth.

"I think it's great. The only thing is, nobody's supposed to wear a letter jacket except lettermen, and I'm not one—not yet."

"This isn't a letter jacket, it's a letter-jacket sweater, and you're well within your rights to wear it," said Elizabeth. She loves to find loopholes in rules.

Victor gave me a box about ten inches by ten inches by ten inches. I opened it up and almost wet my pants.

It was a giant eyeball—at least that's what it looked like. What it really was was a basketball that Victor had painted to look like an eye. It was this white orb with a pupil and a gold-flecked blue iris.

Victor said, "I made it look just like one of your eyes, for identification purposes. Anybody who sees it will know it's yours. What do you think?"

I didn't want to touch it.

Then they blindfolded me and led me down cellar to see their Christmas creation. I could smell pineapple and coconut and hear ocean waves and feel a warm breeze. . . .

Victor lifted off my blindfold, and Elizabeth shouted, "Mele Kalikimaka! It's Christmas in Hawaii!"

They had sound effects and an electric fan blowing scents around and a giant papier-mâché volcano. The volcano rumbled and erupted and zillions of fake flowers shot out of the top of it!

Victor said, "The volcano is like Santa Claus spreading happiness at Christmas." We all picked up handfuls of fake flowers and threw them around.

*　　*　　*

It's hard to top a morning like that, but the afternoon was even better.

I made sure to eat lots of turkey and mashed potatoes and gravy so I'd have a good reason to pass up dessert—pickle pie.

After Victor and I did the dishes, he asked me to give him a hand with something outside. We went out and opened the garage door.

Inside was a backboard with a hoop and a net!

He said, "You're sure you don't mind giving me a hand putting this up?"

"Are you kidding? No way!"

Victor had already cut some lumber to use for supports. He's a good carpenter. We spent the middle of the afternoon on the garage roof with a level and a tape measure and a hammer and nails, putting up the basket, making sure the rim was exactly ten feet off the ground and the backboard was perpendicular to the ground and solid and steady and far enough out from the garage so I could drive in for a layup without bumping into the garage nose first.

It took a lot of work, but finally everything was perfect—or as perfect as it was going to get. You see, the backboard wasn't exactly regulation. It was cut in the shape of the United States. And what's worse, it was a relief map. Victor had attached wooden bumps depicting America's major mountain ranges. He thinks it's important to combine academics with athletics.

I finally dared to pick up the Eye-Ball and give my new homemade basketball court a try. I took a shot from the right side. The ball hit the Appalachian Mountains someplace around West Virginia and bounced back at me.

"Splendid!" said Victor.

It was about three-thirty when I left for the Donovans' house, carrying my new basketball. A little kid was riding a brand-new tricycle in his driveway as I walked past. When he saw the Eye-Ball, he ditched the tricycle and ran into his house crying.

When I got down to the end of the dead end road where Mr. Donovan lives, I remembered what his wife had said about eyes staring at her during the day, and I started to feel scared, but I figured maybe it was just the Eye-Ball giving me the creeps.

Mr. Donovan stepped out onto his back porch when I got to his house. He pointed at the Eye-Ball and said, "Quit staring at me." Oops. I rotated it so it was looking at me. He said, "What's the story, does that ball find its own way into the basket or what?"

"Maybe when *you* shoot it. I don't know about me."

"Let's give it a try."

Mr. Donovan has a nice blacktop court—flat and no ice on it. I took off my mittens and put up a shot. It went in. I guess the Eye-Ball appreciated not bumping into mountains on its way to the hoop.

"Let's play Pig," said Mr. Donovan. "No dotting the *i* or curling the *g* or underlining or punctuation. Just *p-i-g*. Shoot for first shot."

He took a shot and made it. I took one and missed,

so he got to go first. His first shot of the game was a reverse layup. He made it. I missed. Next was a left-handed hook. He made it. I missed. Then he finished me off with a fadeaway jumper. *P-i-g,* just like that.

This is a gracious host?

Well, he *is* gracious. He invited me in for a hot turkey sandwich. Once again, Mrs. Donovan looked pretty happy to have company, and she had plenty of turkey to cut for sandwiches and lots of gravy and everything.

We were still sitting at the kitchen table, almost finished with our pie (*apple,* thank goodness), when there was a noise on the roof. We looked at one another. There it was again. It sounded like footsteps.

Mrs. Donovan said, "What's that?"

"Santa," said Mr. Donovan. "He's here with my big kid who can run and jump and shoot."

"I think it's a robber," she said.

"What's he stealing? Shingles?"

That's when we heard it—a bellow, a bone-chilling "Yeeoww!" from up on the roof, followed by a thump and then the thudding sounds of something tumbling from the chimney to the gutter.

Then I saw something. I'm glad all three of us saw it, because if I'd been the only one, I would have thought it was time for me to go away and lie down quietly for a few years. . . .

The face of a big gorilla had appeared upside down outside the kitchen window over the sink. It was there

31

for only an instant, and then it dropped away, along with its very big dark hairy body.

I looked into Mr. Donovan's eyes, composed myself, and said, "Hibby hibby gogo." I had wanted to say "Let's hide." Before I got another chance to make something comprehensible come out of my mouth, the kitchen door opened—

And it walked in.

It wasn't a gorilla. It was a Bigfoot—a Sasquatch—and it was ten feet away from me and getting closer.

It was eight feet tall (I know that because its head was skimming the ceiling, and the ceilings are eight feet high in Mr. Donovan's house), and it had big ropy shoulders and hands big enough to palm a twenty-five-pound turkey (I know that because it picked up the Donovans' turkey in one hand and put it on the table in front of us).

It was rather slim for a Bigfoot.

It picked up a stool with its free hand, put it down next to the table, and sat looking at us for what seemed like an hour. Its eyes were green with lots of white showing, like a human being's. Its nose was big and lumpy, like Mr. Donovan's. I wondered what it had for teeth, but I hoped I wouldn't find out, because if I did, it might be opening its mouth to eat me up.

It opened its mouth—but only to mutter under its breath, a little like Popeye, but sort of like a baby, too. Maybe it was trying to talk to us, but all I could make out was a bunch of grunts and mumbles and hums.

Then it smiled, and I saw a nice set of choppers, white and even and close together like kernels on an ear of corn. It patted Mr. Donovan on the head, covering him from nose to neck and ear to ear with one hand, a very large hand that looked like a glove— woolly on the outside and leathery on the palm and pads of the fingers. The scene reminded me of a big hairy parent reassuring a big hairy child. Mr. Donovan let out a nervous little laugh.

The more I looked at the Bigfoot, the more it seemed to me that there was something strange about its appearance.

As you probably know, two years ago a team of hot-air balloonists competing in a transatlantic race from Paris, France, to Bangor, Maine, drifted off course near the finish line and crashed in the deep uncharted forest of northern Maine. A Bigfoot family rescued them and nursed them back to health, using secret all-natural remedies.

That was what proved the existence of the Bigfoot. Since then, scientists have tried to learn more about Bigfoots, but it's hard to study them because they like to keep to themselves, and their mastery of camouflage allows them (for the most part) to live in secrecy.

Researchers have managed to determine that Bigfoots mate for life, that they live as long as we do, and that their children mature at about the same rate as we do, but there's still lots to learn. Most of the research has been done on Bigfoot children because they're more trusting of human beings than their parents are. They're also easier to find because they haven't learned all the camouflage tricks yet.

I've watched a couple of Bigfoot specials on PBS and looked at all the pictures in the magazines, but I'd never seen one like this. . . .

"He likes me," said Mr. Donovan. (It was a male. Mr. Donovan is a biology teacher as well as a coach, and he could tell.)

The Bigfoot's grin expanded when Mr. Donovan spoke, and the skin around his eyes got crinkly.

"Of course he likes you," said Mrs. Donovan. "You two could be brothers. I bet he's been hiding in the woods spying on the house because he thinks you're a Bigfoot."

There really *was* a strong resemblance between them. I tried not to laugh, but it wasn't easy. I got sweaty holding the laugh inside. Mrs. Donovan saw me trying to control myself, and she burst out laughing. Then I had to laugh, too.

The Bigfoot did, too. His laugh was really loud, like a honk.

All four of us kept on laughing until Mrs. Donovan sneezed. A quizzical look came over the Bigfoot's face.

Mrs. Donovan sneezed again.

The Bigfoot mimicked her, sticking a finger under his nose, closing his eyes tight, making a face like the Greek mask of tragedy, and letting go with an approximation of "Achoo!"—sort of a "Rooooo!"

34

Mrs. Donovan said, "I'm allergic to dogs, ragweed, and Bigfoots."

That was when I noticed that the Bigfoot smelled like a dog—not bad, just doggy. Probably the only time he really smelled was when he got wet, and I bet the smell wouldn't be all that bad even then because his hair was short, like crew-cut length.

That was why he looked different! He didn't have long hair like other Bigfoots.

While Mrs. Donovan used up a few tissues and the Bigfoot copied her, another thought sprang into my head—this was the "giant bear" Dexter Madison had seen rowing the dinghy. He hung out behind the kilns at night because it was always warm there, and he had wandered far from his home in the north woods because he had such short hair that he couldn't stand the cold weather way up there. That was why he'd taken off for the coast, where the ocean makes the winter milder.

I have to admit I'm a smart guy.

Then the Bigfoot did something that will probably change the course of the whole Down East League basketball season—he picked up the Eye-Ball and walked outside.

Mr. Donovan and I read each other's minds—this Bigfoot would carry the Lawn Ornaments into the tournament and save Mr. Donovan's job! We watched him stand near the basket and take a shot. He missed, but who cared? He's eight feet tall!

Then he tried a reverse layup, a left-handed hook,

and a fadeaway jumper—in that order—and made them.

Mr. Donovan said, "He must have been watching us from the woods. He took the same shots we took in our game of Pig. Picasso, we've found a giant who learns by imitation. He probably learns how to get along in the woods by imitating the other Bigfoots. If we can set a good example for him on the basketball court, he'll turn into the greatest player in the history of Spruce Island Middle School."

"Are you kidding?" I said. "He'll be the greatest player in the history of the whole *league!*"

We cooked up a plan while the Bigfoot played outside. Mr. Donovan said he looked immature, probably about twelve years old, so he'd be the right age to go to our school. We could give him a few days to practice with the Lawn Ornaments during vacation, and then when school started again, he'd be just like one of the regular kids, only bigger and hairier.

Mrs. Donovan said, "He's not living with us. I'm not going to spend the whole basketball season sneezing and blowing my nose with my head all plugged up and my eyes watering and—"

Mr. Donovan said, "But where's he going to live? He has to have an address on the island if he's going to enroll in school."

"Not this address."

Nobody said anything.

When it became clear to me that Mrs. Donovan wasn't going to give in, I said, "I'll call my parents."

I dialed our number. Elizabeth answered.

"Hi, it's me. Elizabeth, is it okay if—a guest—spends the night at our house?"

She squealed, "You've found a friend!" Then she yelled to my father, "Victor sweetie, Picasso has made a little friend!" I choked when I heard her say "little friend."

She talked to me again. "Is he on your team?"

"Um, sort of."

"Well, I'm dying to meet him. Bring him home whenever you're ready."

We loaded the Bigfoot into Mr. Donovan's van and drove to my house. I'm glad it was dark out; the neighbors didn't see the Bigfoot as he walked with us from the van to the house.

Victor met us at the back door, took one look at the Bigfoot, and fainted. He was out cold on the kitchen floor when Elizabeth ran to him, saw the Bigfoot filling the doorway, and passed out, too. The Bigfoot got down on the floor next to them and lay down flat with a big grin on his face, happy to be included in what he apparently thought was a game.

Our kitchen reminded me of Custer's Last Stand.

Victor and Elizabeth came to eventually, and we explained about the Bigfoot. Mr. Donovan made sure everybody was okay and then he went home, leaving us Dewlaps alone with our very large guest.

My parents got used to the Bigfoot right away. (They had a variety of unusual friends in Chicago.)

Elizabeth took the Bigfoot by the hand—make that "by the finger"—and led him on a tour of the house, telling him what we do in all the rooms. Even though he didn't understand her, he seemed to like the gentle sound of her voice.

Not many mothers would be so nice to a Bigfoot.

When we got down cellar, the Bigfoot got a load of the "Christmas in Hawaii" installation and did a happy little dance and clapped his hands. I watched him close his eyes and let the warm breeze and tropical aromas wash over him. Then he let out a big sigh and lay down on some fake flowers near the volcano.

This was the perfect place for a short-haired Bigfoot who can't stand the cold. He mumbled happily and fell sound asleep.

December 26

●————————————

*H*awaiian music woke me up. I followed it to the cellar, where I found Victor and Elizabeth dancing the hula with the Bigfoot. It looked pretty stupid, but they were laughing and everything, so I danced with them, and it was fun—but still stupid.

All that wiggling gave us a good appetite for breakfast. The Bigfoot ate a pint of vanilla yogurt, four apples, and six bowls of Neato-Wheatos. For dessert he devoured a pickle pie.

As I cleared the table, I heard a beep-beep from the driveway. It was Mr. Donovan. I went outside to see if anybody was watching—nobody was.

We hustled the Bigfoot into the van and hit the road for school. Mr. Donovan said, "Mrs. Dingley is going to meet us in the office." She's the school secretary.

"How much does she know?"

"Not much. All she knows is she's going to enroll a new basketball player. She'll do anything to help the Lawn Ornaments make the tournament, even if it means working on the day after Christmas."

We parked behind the school. Mr. Donovan used his key to open one of the back doors. It felt funny walking through the corridors when there were no kids around, and having a Bigfoot accompany us didn't make things seem more natural.

Mrs. Dingley was sitting at her desk putting an enrollment form into her typewriter when the three of us walked into the office. I thought she'd have a heart attack when she saw the Bigfoot, but all she did was say, "Pupil's name?"

Oops. What *was* his name? How come we didn't think of that? He had to have a name—

"Ed Tibbetts," I said.

I have no idea where that name came from. I don't know anybody by that name. I didn't really even think of the name—it just sort of came out of my mouth uninvited.

"Ed Tibbetts," she repeated as she typed his name on the form.

I gave Ed's age as twelve, relying on Mr. Donovan's judgment, and our address as Ed's legal residence. Mrs. Dingley finished typing, stood up, and stuck out her hand to shake with Ed. "Welcome to Spruce Island Middle School, home of the Lawn Ornaments." Ed shook her hand gently and smiled. Then we left the office.

I couldn't believe how cool Mrs. Dingley was! You'd think she enrolled Bigfoots every day!

We walked to the locker room. Ed was peeking in all the classrooms and looking at all the bulletin boards on the way. While Mr. Donovan searched through his ring of keys for the one that opened the coaches' room, I heard something outside in the corridor.

It was Mrs. Dingley sprinting at what sounded like top speed and yelling, "Big and hairy! Big and hairy!" over and over until she was outside.

We stayed in the coaches' room until the other guys arrived for practice. Then I went out to the locker room to change while Mr. Donovan kept Ed out of sight.

One by one we went out onto the gym floor and shot around. I thought about telling Dexter that he was right about the giant bear rowing the dinghy, only it was a Bigfoot, but I didn't dare. He'd know soon enough anyway.

Mr. Donovan joined us. He said, "A new player is going to join our team today. His name is Ed Tibbetts, and he's living with the Dewlap family. I want you to make him feel at home, okay?" Roland made some crack that I didn't catch. "Now here he is—Ed Tibbetts."

Ed came out, and ten guys ran the other way screaming. Only Dexter, Mr. Donovan, and I stayed put. All the screaming must have scared Ed; he ran to the other end of the gym and sat in the corner trembling.

"Come back here, you guys," said Mr. Donovan. "He's not going to hurt you."

The Lawn Ornaments walked toward us slowly, keeping an eye on Ed.

Mr. Donovan said, "Ed learns by imitating what he sees—it's Bigfoot see, Bigfoot do. So I want you to practice as you always do, only better, and show him how to play basketball right. Okay?"

A few guys said okay, but I could barely hear them. I took a look at Ed in the corner. He seemed pretty upset. Then all of a sudden he got up and ran right at the Lawn Ornaments—and slipped and fell! You should have seen the guys scatter! He got to his feet and kept running (and sliding) to the door and went outside.

I followed him outside and found him on his hands and knees. He had thrown up his breakfast, and, for a change, I think the cause was a nervous stomach rather than my mother's pickle pie.

I got him calmed down, and he went back inside with me and watched practice from the bench. It would be nice to report that we played better than usual, but we didn't.

Roland had a good day, though. I think he was inspired by the prospect of playing with an eight-foot-tall center. Our regular center, O. O'Malley, spent the whole practice peering over his shoulder to make sure Ed wasn't stalking him.

Big and Hairy

Dexter didn't say a word to anybody during practice or afterward in the locker room. If I had been the one who'd been laughed at for saying he'd seen a giant bear rowing a dinghy, I would have been saying, "I told you so" to everybody, but he just kept to himself.

He's an unusual guy.

December 27

---

*E*d sat by himself on the bench, knees up around his ears, and watched us practice. I think he was just starting to get used to being with us when the gym doors flew open and a million newspaper reporters burst in, pointing at him and yelling and carrying on like nuts. Ed tumbled off the bench and took off for the locker room, slipping and sliding all the way. (His feet are slippery, like socks on the gym floor.)

Mr. Donovan followed Ed to the locker room and stood guard outside the door to keep the reporters away from him. I'd never seen him so mad.

"Get out of here!" he yelled.

The reporters kept coming.

"You're scaring him!"

They kept coming.

"No street shoes allowed on the gym floor!"

That got them. I guess some lessons we learn in school stick with us all our lives.

Mr. Donovan spread his arms and herded the reporters toward the doors. Roland grabbed a ball out of my hands and showed off for them, spinning the ball on his index finger and dribbling behind his back and between his legs.

I'm sure the reporters were very impressed.

When we were in the locker room after practice, Mr. Gimpwater, the principal, came in. His toupee took on a greenish tinge under the fluorescent lights. When he saw Mr. Donovan, he smiled like that guy who hosts "Bowling for Bait."

"Mr. Donovan," he said, "it has come to my attention that you have a Bigfoot on your team."

"So what?" said Mr. Donovan. He was still mad.

"I was thinking you might want to hold a press conference to introduce him to the public."

"Why?"

Mr. Gimpwater's smile faded away. He looked at Mr. Donovan's feet. "Um—because Mr. Bumstock says you should."

"I see."

"Good. Two o'clock at Rodney's." Mr. Gimpwater showed his teeth again and left.

I got to Rodney's at five minutes before two. The place was filled with reporters—five times as many as there'd been at the gym (they'd come in from all over)—and Rodney was running out of food. Mr. Bumstock was making a speech about the "twin glories" of Spruce Island: basketball and Bumstock lawn ornaments. The reporters were ignoring him, but the islanders were listening, even though they'd heard his speech a thousand times already.

Mr. Donovan arrived bundled up in a heavy overcoat and knit cap with a scarf wrapped around his face. It was freezing cold outside. A reporter—evidently one of the newcomers who hadn't been there in time to see Ed at the gym—mistook him for Ed and yelled, "Run for your lives!"

The reporters and photographers stampeded, some toward Mr. Donovan, some away.

"Relax," he said as he took off his scarf, "I'm only the coach."

Right away all the reporters started shouting out questions at the same time. (I've always thought that looked phony in movies, but I guess it's the way they do it.)

I could tell Mr. Donovan was still mad. He said, "If you can all keep your traps shut for a minute, I'll tell you everything."

And he did. It was all stuff you've already read, so I'm not going to make you read it again.

All the Lawn Ornaments were there—except Ed—and we posed for a team picture after Mr. Donovan finished making his statement to the press.

A reporter from Channel Thirteen in Portland said, "Which one is the Dewlap boy?"

I raised my hand. (No, I didn't say "present.")

She said, "How does it feel to be the first boy to see the Bigfoot?"

How do you tell anybody how something *feels?*

What a dopey question. I got off the hook by telling the truth. I said, "I wasn't the first boy to see Ed. Dexter Madison was." Then I pointed at Dexter. I knew he'd hate talking to the press, but I figured he wouldn't kill me with all these witnesses on hand.

The reporters gathered around him, and he told them about seeing Ed rowing the dinghy, and then he shut up. The interview lasted twelve seconds.

I had a feeling he was going to rub me out when he got the opportunity. I didn't want to look at him, but I had to check if he was doing anything like pulling a derringer out of his boot or something—so I looked at him.

And he smiled at me.

Boy, was I confused. Before I could sort things out, Elizabeth walked in and made her way through the crowd to the counter. "Is it all over?" she asked Rodney.

Rodney said, "I guess so. I don't have any more food for them anyway."

"Really?" said Elizabeth. "I could run home and get a few pickle pies." Then she turned to the reporters and said in a loud voice, "Anyone for pickle pie?"

That ended the press conference. My mother knows how to clear a room.

Mr. Bumstock said, "Time for the photo opportunity. The Bigfoot is waiting for you at the Bumstock Lawn Ornament Company, maker of America's finest ceramic gewgaws since 1915!"

We all nearly froze as we walked up the hill from

the waterfront to the factory. I tried to catch Dexter's eye to see if he'd smile again, but I couldn't. Maybe I'd imagined the smile. Maybe he had gas. I don't know.

Mr. Bumstock told the photographers where they should set up to get the best angle on Ed and the Bumstock sign on the roof. Then he walked up the granite steps to the front door of the factory with Mr. Donovan and went in. A moment later they opened the heavy wooden door and stepped out with Victor and Ed.

Most of the reporters and photographers gasped, but one of them said, "That's no Bigfoot, it's a fake. Where's his long hair?"

Mr. Bumstock said, "I assure you, Ed Tibbetts is a *gen-yoo-ine* Bigfoot, and Ludlow Bumstock knows whereof he speaks."

The reporter said, "Make him take off that dress so we can get a good look at him and decide for ourselves."

Ed wasn't wearing a dress. It was a poncho Elizabeth had made for him from two blankets, and it was the best thing for a short-haired Bigfoot to wear on the coldest day of the winter. Victor reluctantly helped him take it off.

Right away Ed started to shiver. I felt sorry for him. He looked like some naked kid standing on a cold linoleum floor in a doctor's office.

Maybe I'm reading too much into the expression I

saw on Ed's face, but I think he felt like a freak, the poor guy.

Mr. Bumstock said to the reporter, "Come up here close and see for yourself."

I could tell the reporter didn't dare to, but he couldn't look like a chicken in front of the others, so he climbed the steps—slowly. When he got to the top, he lifted his head for the first time and looked up at Ed for one thousandth of a second, spun on his heel, ran down the steps, and said, "That's a Bigfoot."

December 28

The headline on the front page of the *Rocky Coast Blabber* said, "Spruce Island Welcomes Big Hairy Lawn Ornament." I started to read the story and had just seen my name in print for the first time in my life when Elizabeth shrieked and poked Victor in the ribs and pointed at the portable TV on the kitchen counter.

We were on TV! There we were on "Hey, Wake Up!" with the president of Egypt and Jimmy the Ice-Skating Dog and the Jolly Weatherman and everybody! Victor and I shrieked, too.

The noise woke up Ed, who ran upstairs from the "Christmas in Hawaii" room and slipped on the kitchen floor. He took a look at the TV, saw himself standing at the door of the factory, got excited, and bellowed "Aaooh! Aaaoooh!" He did it again, and all three of us bellowed with him. The window over the sink rattled, and dishes clinked in the cupboard.

After a few minutes we calmed down enough to finish breakfast. Then we left for practice.

It's not easy to walk with a Bigfoot. I had to move along at a pace just slightly slower than a run, sort of like somebody who has to get to the rest room fast but doesn't want anybody to know.

A voice called out, "Dewlap!"

I froze. It was Dexter Madison, the silent guy ready to crack, the man on the edge, the poster boy for juvenile ax murder. He said, "Wait up."

I grabbed Ed by the arm and waited to meet my fate. He caught up with us and said, "Mind if I walk with you?"

"Uh, no. Not at all. Sure. Why not? Of course. Be my guest."

We walked for a while without talking. I was nervous. Then Dexter said, "Thanks for telling them I was the first one to see Ed. It was kind of fun to see the reporters write down what I said. They were really listening to me, and they didn't think I was stupid or crazy."

"You know, I should have told you this a long time ago—I had a feeling you were right about Ed rowing the dinghy, because I found his footprint behind the ovens at the factory the next day."

"You did? Why didn't you tell me?"

"I guess I was afraid to."

"How come?"

"You seemed kind of mad at everybody."

"I wasn't mad at *you.* You've never made fun of me."

"I thought you wanted to pound me for blowing the game."

"That day in the locker room? All I wanted to do was tell you not to worry about it, but you ran away."

"I guess that was pretty stupid."

"Wicked stupid," said Dexter. Then he grinned at me.

I felt great. Dexter and Ed and I ran the rest of the way to school.

When we got to the locker room we saw Mr. Bumstock walking out of the coaches' room with a big smile on his face and his skinny old arm halfway around Mr. Donovan's back. He was saying, "Yes, I think I misjudged you. You do know how to win."

Mr. Donovan said, "But using a Bigfoot—"

"Is brilliant. Brilliant!" said Mr. Bumstock. "And stop worrying about playing fair. Just win." Then he left, whistling. Mr. Donovan went back into the coaches' room, shut the door, and stayed in there until practice started.

Ed stayed on the bench during practice and watched us. I wonder if he's learning much about how to play basketball. Maybe it's confusing for him to watch so many people running around at the same time. But even if he knew what to do on the court, he couldn't have played because his feet would have slipped too much.

We're going to have to do something about those feet if Ed's ever going to play with us.

I noticed a man standing at the door looking around the gym. He had a piece of paper in his hand. I guess he was looking for Mr. Donovan, because he walked toward him really fast all of a sudden. When he got closer to me, I recognized him. I didn't know his name, but I knew he was the Rockweed Harbor Middle School basketball coach.

"Coach Donovan," he said, "I hear you've got a Bigfoot on your team."

Mr. Donovan said, "I think the whole country has heard. Want to meet him?"

"No, thanks. And I don't want to meet him in a basketball game, either. It's not fair to have an eight-foot-tall animal playing against a bunch of kids, and you know it. I won't stand for it."

"Oh, you won't, huh? Well, you can't tell me what to do."

"Maybe I can't, but I've filed a complaint with the Maine Athletic Directors' Association. *They* can tell you what to do." He gave the piece of paper to Mr. Donovan. "It's all spelled out here. Show up at the hearing tomorrow—and say good-bye to your big, hairy Lawn Ornament."

December 29

———————●———————

I stayed awake most of the night reading the league rule book and trying to think of a loophole that would allow Ed to play for us, but I didn't come up with anything.

At two o'clock in the afternoon, I was sitting in our school's conference room waiting for the rules committee of the Maine Athletic Directors' Association to show up. Steam was hissing in the old radiators, and the heat was making me sleepy. Ed took off his poncho, made a pillow of it, and lay down.

Mr. Donovan and the coach from Rockweed Harbor were sitting next to each other, staring straight ahead, not saying a word. The Rockweed coach looked mad, and Mr. Donovan looked worried. He was fiddling with his beard.

The rules committee finally showed up. It looked as though the chairman had been dragged away from a day of ice fishing. He sat down and peeled off a few layers of clothes.

The Rockweed Harbor coach spoke first. He whined about how unfair it was for us to have a Bigfoot on our team when nobody else did. The committee listened and nodded.

When it was our turn, Mr. Donovan talked about how gentle Ed is, how he'd never hurt a fly, even though he's a huge wild animal who could rip the tailgate off a pickup truck if he wanted to. I tell you, the more he talked about how gentle Ed is, the more dangerous he made him sound.

The committee members glanced nervously at Ed, who was still sleeping. Mr. Donovan must have figured out how they felt, because he changed his line and went on about how Ed was a legal resident of Spruce Island and the proper age for middle school and duly enrolled and shouldn't be deprived of the joy of interacting with students his own age. He sounded quite official.

I guess the Rockweed Harbor coach got worried, because he stood up and said the rule book made no provisions for wild animals.

He had a point.

I could tell Mr. Donovan thought we'd lost. I thought so, too.

Then it hit me. I guess listening to Elizabeth find legal loopholes all these years (like my letter-jacket sweater) has paid off.

I said, "I'd like to say something," and I kept on

talking before the chairman had a chance to tell me to be quiet. "It seems to me this committee wants to go strictly by the rule book. Well, I've read it, and as far as I can see, it refers to male and female athletes. Period. It doesn't refer to species. And Ed Tibbetts is a male athlete—a male Bigfoot athlete, but a male athlete just the same."

The committee members consulted their rule books. Finally the chairman said, "You're right. He qualifies."

Mr. Donovan and I cheered.

The Rockweed Harbor coach sputtered, "You can't let a Bigfoot play in the Down East League against kids!"

"We have to," said the chairman. "We have to go by the book."

"Change the book," said the Rockweed coach.

"We will," said the chairman, "next year. But for this season, the ruling stands."

Mr. Donovan and I woke Ed up, helped him get dressed, and walked him to the front door of the school. My heart was pounding. I couldn't believe I had spoken up like that.

You should have seen the crowd outside! I think every islander who wasn't needed at the factory was there to hear the verdict.

I caught Mrs. Donovan's eye and winked at her discreetly. I hope she didn't think I was being fresh. The wink was just my way of letting her know we had won. Besides, I was proud that I'd saved the day, and I felt like winking.

Mr. Donovan and I raised Ed's arms and shook our fists. The crowd cheered like mad!

Some islanders pumped Mrs. Donovan's hand and told her how good it was to have a coach who understood how important it is for the Lawn Ornaments to make the tournament. She looked awfully happy.

December 30

We played well at practice today. I think officially having Ed on our team is making us better. Now that we know he's really going to play with us, we're trying harder to set a good example for him so he'll learn how to play right.

It's kind of funny to watch Ed watch us play. His forehead gets wrinkly and he squints a little, sort of like a kid doing algebra. I guess what's funny is that he looks so human.

(That's a human-chauvinist-pig thing to say, isn't it? Who's to say Ed looks human? He probably thinks we look Bigfootian.)

At the end of practice, Mr. Donovan said, "You guys were great today. I think you gave Ed a good idea of how to play every position and how each player's duties fit into the big picture. I'm proud of you. You played as a team."

We all felt good. I tried to look mature. Mr. Donovan went on, "Now, as soon as we get a pair of sneakers big enough for Ed, we'll see how much he's learned."

I walked home with Ed and Dexter. Dexter came in and played Chinese checkers with me. Ed watched. I don't think he figured out how to play, but even if he did, I think he would have had trouble moving the little marbles around with his big, meaty fingers.

I asked Dexter to stay for lunch, but he had to go because the tide was going out and he had to dig some clams on the flats.

In the afternoon Ed and I were watching "The Three Stooges" on TV when the doorbell rang. I opened the door and almost dropped dead. Some kids from school had come by to visit!

They stayed until it was getting dark—watching TV, making the volcano in Ed's room spew fake flowers, goofing around with Ed, making faces at him and getting him to make them back at them—you know, stuff like that. I had a blast!

I joined the basketball team to make friends, but, boy, I never thought I'd be this lucky.

January 2

⸻

Elizabeth has sewn some clothes for Ed to wear to school, cotton outfits, like what doctors wear in the operating room.

"Calling Dr. Tibbetts. Dr. Ed Tibbetts to ICU."

He put on his red one this morning and took off with me for his first day of school. There were no extra desks in my homeroom, and Mrs. Frappier, the teacher, wasn't there yet, so I took Ed to Mr. Gimpwater's office to see about getting him a desk. He's way too big for a regular one, so we took a table—that is, Ed took it. He carried it under his right arm. He carried a chair under his left, and back we went to homeroom.

Mrs. Frappier had arrived. She was talking to some girls, saying how much fun she and her husband had had on their Christmas vacation in the Caribbean and how they had just come back last night and, yes, it did feel funny to have a tan in the middle of winter, and, no, she hadn't heard the big news about the new kid in school—and then Ed banged his table against the doorjamb on his way into the room.

Mrs. Frappier saw him and lost her tan.

But we had a good day. Ed sat quietly near me during my classes and, as the day went on, knocked over fewer and fewer people with his table and chair when we changed rooms.

Victor and Elizabeth had given me enough money to buy one lunch for myself and three for Ed. The school lunch today was a scoop of mashed potatoes stuck inside a piece of bologna that was curled up like a cup, lima beans, a wheat roll and butter, chilled milk, and stewed prunes for dessert. I didn't have any trouble finishing my lunch in the seventeen minutes they give us, but Ed had to hustle to eat three.

Twenty minutes into social studies, I could tell Ed wasn't feeling good. He slumped in his seat and moaned. He put his head on the table. He rubbed his belly. Nothing he did made him feel any better. When he looked at me, he was sweating, and his eyes seemed to say, "Please help me."

I took the poor guy to the boys' room, showed him where everything was, and then waited outside in the hall. Immediately I heard grunting. It went on for almost a minute. Then Ed began to howl.

He kept it up long enough to attract the attention of Mr. Gimpwater and the teachers who were spending their free period in the teachers' lounge.

"What's going on?" said Mr. Gimpwater.

"Ed's lunch didn't agree with him," I said.

"Can't you get him to stop that howling?"

"Maybe, but I'd rather not try."

One of the teachers said, "You go in, Larry." (I think it's funny when teachers forget there's a kid around and call each other by their first names.)

Larry—er, Mr. Gimpwater—said, "Perhaps we should allow him his privacy."

That was smart; a foul odor was escaping the boys' room.

Before long, I could hear Ed flush the toilet, pump the soap dispenser, and step on the foot rail to start the big fountain-style faucet in the round sink. A moment later he reappeared clean and refreshed.

In the locker room after school Ed put on a gym suit that Elizabeth had made for him. It was just like his school clothes, only the bottoms were shorts and the shirt was a tank top. Elizabeth thought he'd feel more like a Lawn Ornament if he wore something that looked like a uniform, even though he couldn't actually get out on the court with us until he had a pair of sneakers.

He didn't have to wait long.

A representative from the Ounces of Bounces Sneaker Company—the brand pros like me wear—was standing in the gym next to a photographer, with two pairs of huge high-top sneakers. When he saw Ed, he elbowed the photographer and shouted, "Ed! Hey, Ed baby! Over here for a minute, my man!" His dazzling smile made me think he had some Gimpwater blood somewhere in his family history.

He made Ed hold a sneaker and pose with him for the photographer. It seemed to me that the blinding flashes and the representative's loud, grabby personality were bothering Ed, but before I got a chance to complain on his behalf, the representative left him alone and said, "That'll do it, Ed. Marvelous working with you. Lunch soon."

Maybe it's my imagination, but I thought I saw a funny look in Ed's eyes when the representative mentioned lunch. Anyway, the whole photo session was over before we knew what had hit us.

Ed showed me a piece of paper the representative had stuck in his hand on the way out. It was a press release telling about the sneakers. "A white pair for home games, green for away," it said. "Size 38 EEEEEE. The finest Bigfoot basketball sneakers ever produced in the state of Maine." It went on to describe how the sneakers had turned an "unskilled animal" into "an unstoppable scoring machine." Pretty persuasive advertising, huh? Especially considering Ed had never played a game in his life or even laced up a sneaker.

I guess somebody at the Ounces of Bounces company got an A in creative writing.

Ed put on two pairs of homemade white socks. I

got him started lacing up one of the sneakers, and then I flipped over its mate and looked at the sole. It was similar to the tread on my Ounces of Bounces, but the tread on mine spells "jump" on the left one and "run" on the right. Ed's left one is big enough to say "Jump higher than you've ever jumped previously!" The tread on the right one says, "Run fast like a bunny rabbit! Really!"

It was time for Ed to show what he could do.

O. O'Malley walked up to him and shook his hand solemnly. "Darned pleased to have you aboard," he said.

I think he was hoping Ed would take over his position at center and give him a chance to stay outside and shoot from the O Zone.

Mr. Donovan took a ball off the rack and showed Ed how to dunk with one hand and with two hands. We were impressed.

Then he gave the ball to Ed, and we looked on in awe.

Ed stood flat-footed and dunked with his right, his left, and both hands. After about twenty dunks, he looked bored.

Mr. Donovan was panting and drooling like that beagle in the dog food commercial. When he had calmed down enough to speak, he said, "Roland and O., help me show Ed how to play center on defense."

Roland played guard. Mr. Donovan played center, and O. guarded him. He stayed close to Mr. Donovan and kept between him and the basket. Mr. Donovan passed the ball out to Roland, and of course Roland shot.

O. turned around fast to face the basket. He made sure he kept Mr. Donovan away from the basket. When the ball rolled off the rim, O. jumped for it and caught it with two hands.

Mr. Donovan said, "O., that was perfect. Ed couldn't ask for a better role model."

O. ducked his head. He was probably embarrassed. I couldn't see if he had turned red because his hair had fallen over his face and was hanging down to his chin.

Mr. Donovan said, "Now let's see if the big boy was paying attention."

Mr. Donovan took over for Roland. O. played offense and Ed played defense—sort of. Mr. Donovan threw a bounce pass toward O. O. reached for it. So did Ed.

They tried again. This time, O. spun around and ran across the lane. Ed spun around and ran across the lane with him. O. cut toward the basket and slipped. Ed cut toward the basket and slipped with him.

"Uh-oh," said Mr. Donovan. "Looks like Ed hasn't quite grasped the concept of defense."

It was true. Instead of trying to keep his man from scoring, Ed was doing whatever his man was doing. Oh, brother.

(Hey, what if Ed's man punched Roland in the nose? Hmm . . .)

Mr. Donovan said, "Ed, I want you to rethink this defense business, okay? We'll work on it and practice hard, and you'll be just fine by game time on Friday."

Fine by Friday?

I guess it's okay for a coach to tell fibs to a player who can't understand what he's saying.

January 6

———————•———————

During the game the gym was so full that the fire department had to close the doors to keep some people out. Rodney opened her café for them. Too bad; she wanted to go to the game, too, because it was Ed's basketball debut.

Our opponent was Potato Head Middle School. The first time I heard that name, I pictured a school full of tiny plastic students with missing parts. Then I found out that Potato Head is the name of a cape up the coast where they grow potatoes. They should have called it Cape Potato or Potato Promontory or something, but I guess they were growing potatoes there before anybody ever thought of making a game of building a little potato man.

Anyway, people were crammed into every inch of sitting and standing space. Photographers sat cross-legged along the baselines. When I scanned the crowd,

I saw Victor and Elizabeth swaying and clapping to the music of the pep band. Mr. Gimpwater was there, delivering a box of popcorn and a soda to Mr. Bumstock. They were sitting with the rules committee of the Maine Athletic Directors' Association.

Islanders patted Mr. Donovan on the back when they passed behind the bench on their way in. Somebody had given Mrs. Donovan a corsage. It was a big night.

Ed was on the bench when the game started. Some of our fans booed. They had wanted to see him play right away. They didn't complain long, though, because we jumped out to a big lead without him. I guess concentrating at practice on showing Ed how to play properly paid off. And besides, the Potato Head Misters (they couldn't resist) had a hard time keeping their minds on what they were doing. They kept checking our bench to make sure Ed was still there and not chasing after them licking his chops.

Mr. Donovan put me in when we were leading 10 to 2. It was fun to play when I didn't have to worry about losing the game for us and getting run off the island. We were playing so well that I knew the Misters didn't have a chance of beating us—and still we hadn't used our not-so-secret weapon. . . .

Mr. Donovan put Ed in at the start of the second quarter. I expected the crowd to stand up and cheer and stomp on the bleachers, but they were silent. I guess the sight of Ed out there on the court wearing his white high-tops and his almost-official uniform (made by Elizabeth), standing in the midst of four normal-size kids (us) and five normal-size kids who were scared stiff (them), could make anybody quiet.

Ed set up just outside the lane with his back to the basket. He was in a good post-up position, so we applauded for him. Three Misters guarded him, but it looked to me as if they didn't want to get too close. I passed the ball to him. The Misters cleared out. Ed pivoted, took a step, and dunked effortlessly with his left hand. We applauded.

The crowd was still quiet. I guess it's hard to cheer when you're speechless.

We ran to the other end of the court and set up our two-three zone defense. When you're on defense, you can stay in the lane as long as you want without getting called for a three-second violation. Ed stood in front of the basket and held his arms up. We gave him a nice round of applause.

A Mister made a halfhearted attempt to lure Ed away from the basket by running at him and then running away from him. It didn't work. Ed stayed put, and we clapped.

The Misters had a pretty good idea they couldn't drive successfully on Ed, so one of them took a shot from outside. As the ball came down, Ed reached up and caught it just as it was about to go in.

Tweeet! Ed was called for goaltending. You can't touch the ball when it's on its way down if it has a chance to go in. The shot counted as a basket for Potato Head.

We all shook our heads and clucked our tongues at Ed like fussy old ladies who disapprove of nasty language in movies. Ed looked sheepish. (Am I mixing my species?)

Here's the story—this past week we helped Mr. Donovan train Ed to do the right thing on the court. He says what we're doing is behavior modification. When Ed does something right, like taking a shot instead of mimicking the guy who's guarding him, we clap. That's positive reinforcement. When he does the wrong thing—even if it's not a foul—we do the head-shake-and-cluck routine (negative reinforcement) and hope that he cuts it out before the other team takes advantage of what he's doing or the ref calls something on him.

This time down the court, Ed evidently forgot we had the ball and stood in the middle of the lane as if he were on defense. I could see the official counting to himself, "One . . . two . . ." I clucked and shook like crazy, and Ed jumped out of the lane before the count of three. He's quite nimble.

We gave him a nice hand.

I suppose one of us kids could have driven in for an easy shot, because Ed was triple-teamed, and even the two Misters who weren't guarding him were keeping an uneasy eye on him, but I think we were all more interested in seeing what Ed could do. Dexter tossed the ball high in his direction. Before we got a chance to clap, Ed jumped up—his chin was above the rim—caught the ball, and slammed it through the hoop and net with both hands. The whole thing was kind of *whoosh! blam!*—like a bomb going off inside a tornado.

We applauded like mad, and the islanders did, too. Ed knew he had done the right thing, and he grinned at us and waved to the crowd as he scampered down to the other end of the court.

The Misters didn't look happy.

We ended up winning 72 to 15. We could have scored more points, but Mr. Donovan continued his policy of substituting players frequently, and Ed sat on the bench some of the time. He still got forty-eight points and thirty rebounds.

I scored six points, and Roland didn't say one nasty thing to me.

There was a big celebration in the locker room after the game. Ed and the rest of us turned our radios up loud and snapped towels at one another. (We really know how to live.) The only one who didn't take part was Dexter. He changed quickly and left. I figured something was bugging him, but I didn't know what.

The celebration moved on to Rodney's. It was so crowded there I could barely squeeze through the door.

A TV news crew about twenty feet from me turned on some bright lights and started shooting an interview with Mr. Donovan. They had him standing next to Ed, who was sitting at the counter eating his free hamburgers. I tried to work my way closer to the action, but I didn't get far.

The scene reminded me of election night TV coverage, with reporters in hotel ballrooms asking winners how it feels while happy people stand around making noise, except nobody at Rodney's was wearing a funny hat. People were happy, though. Victor and Elizabeth were waving at me from across the room, and all I could do was wave back because I didn't stand a chance of getting to them through the crowd. Mr. Bumstock was looking satisfied as he chatted with the chairman of the rules committee, and Mr. Gimpwater was happy because Mr. Bumstock was happy.

Really, all that grinning could make you gag.

I heard Mr. Donovan answering a question. I could tell he was having fun sounding like a big-time coach. He said, "We're very happy to have Ed on our team. He has all the tools you like to see in a big man, and he also has a fine work ethic. Now it's just a matter of finding the right combinations of players to complement his talent in the different situations we face."

The interviewer said, "Any problem with the other players getting jealous of the big guy?"

"None at all," said Mr. Donovan. "In fact, having Ed on the team allows me to give more playing time to some of our kids who need a little experience. Ed makes the other twelve boys better players. . . ."

I saw a funny look cross Mr. Donovan's face when he said "the other twelve boys." I didn't figure out what the problem was right away, but I felt that familiar sinking feeling in my stomach.

"Hold on!" shouted the chairman of the rules committee. "I've got something to say, and you're not going to like it."

The room got quiet.

"You know, in all the excitement over having a Bigfoot play basketball in our league, I overlooked an infraction of the rules. Coach Donovan, you have thirteen players on your team, and the rules state clearly that you are allowed no more than twelve. I'm sorry to say that Potato Head wins by forfeit."

Two hundred forty-five people gasped at once, causing a temporary shortage of oxygen in the room.

The chairman went on to say, "I'm afraid you can't use Ed Tibbetts—unless you get rid of one of the other players."

Just then I felt somebody squeeze the pressure point in my arm right above my elbow. It was Roland LeMay. He tightened his grip until the nerve was killing me. Then he put his ugly mouth close to my ear and whispered, "Turn in your uniform."

January 7

I have to quit.

I suppose somebody else could quit, but the other guys are all better than I am and they've all lived here longer than I have, so I really ought to be the one. Besides, if I don't quit, Roland LeMay will rip out my guts and feed them to the seagulls.

It's pretty weird—I joined the team so I could make friends, but now if I stay on the team, everyone will hate me because I'll be keeping Ed off the team. If Ed doesn't play, the Lawn Ornaments won't make the tournament and Mr. Donovan will get fired and he won't be able to get another coaching job because no school is going to want to hire a coach who got fired.

I did all this thinking in bed last night. I don't like what I've decided, but it's the only thing for me to do.

I have to quit.

January 8

━━━━━━━━━━━━━●━━━━━━━━━━━━━

Dexter took Ed and me out to Sheep Island in his dinghy to dig some clams at low tide. The sun was bright on the water, and there was some warmth in the breeze.

On our way out, Dexter asked me what kind of a name Picasso is. I told him I'm named for Pablo Picasso, the famous artist. He said he'd never heard of him.

Some people seem proud to say they've never heard of somebody, as if being ignorant makes them superior to the person they've never heard of, but Dexter isn't like that. He just stated a fact. That's why I don't think he's stupid. I think he just hasn't found out some stuff yet. Everybody's uninformed about something. Take me, for instance. Before today, I didn't know anything about clamming.

When we put the boat ashore on the east side of

the island, I looked out across the open ocean, and the sky was so clear it seemed as if I could watch TV in Europe if somebody over there would just throw open the drapes. It was a perfect day, but only Ed enjoyed it.

Something was still bothering Dexter, and I didn't feel so hot, either, but neither of us talked about what was bugging us. We walked to his favorite clamming spot.

The tides are really big in Maine. When the tide is low, acres of wet sand and rocks are exposed. Dexter showed me how to look for little bubbles coming out of pinholes in the wet sand. If you dig down with the clam hoe where the bubbles are, you'll find clams.

Ed wasn't interested, so Dexter let him row the boat.

After we had dug for a while and filled up the clam hod (that's a wooden basket), I said, "Dexter, I want to tell you something. I'm quitting the team."

"Are you sure you want to?"

"Yuh, I'm sure. It's kind of selfish of me to stay on and keep Ed off. He was born to play basketball."

"No, he wasn't. He was born to live a Bigfoot life with other Bigfoots. It's not fair to have him on our team. It's not fair to the other teams, and it's not fair to Ed."

"What do you mean not fair to Ed?"

"We're using him. Only thing anybody cares about is winning stupid basketball games, and nobody cares about Ed."

"But he likes basketball."

"He likes rowing my boat, too, but I'm not hiring him to take me around. He's like a big baby, Picasso, and he'll do anything. He don't know any better."

I looked out at the cove and saw Ed rowing around in big circles and bellowing something that sounded like "Toot toot!"

Dexter said, "Quit if you want to, but take Ed with you."

I was getting mad. "You're just jealous because he gets more rebounds than you do."

Dexter kept cool. "I don't like people looking at Ed like something in a freak show at a fair."

"They don't think that. They think he's great. They like him—"

"Because they're selfish. When we win, they think they're great, and when he plays, we win. That's part of the reason they like him. But the other part is because he's just so big. Deep down inside, they're laughing at him because they think he's a freak and they think they're not, and that makes them feel good."

"You don't know what you're talking about."

"I do, too," said Dexter. "Guys like Roland think I'm stupid and they laugh at me because it makes them feel like they're something special. I don't like it, and I don't want to see Ed get treated that way."

January 27

———————●———————

I took a look at the entries in my journal and noticed that since January 9 I've been whining about how I don't fit in on the island and how the kids at school are crazy about Ed but they've forgotten me and how the islanders don't appreciate the sacrifice I made to keep Ed on the team—and, oh, boo-hoo-hoo, it's just so sad.

I'll spare you.

Instead, here's a little summary of other stuff I've written down. At the end of it, I'm going to tell you some bad news and then some weird news.

Mr. Donovan told me I didn't have to quit, that in fairness Ed should be the one to quit because he joined the team after I did, but I said my mind was made up. He said the team would miss me.

I have a feeling they'd miss Ed more.

Big and Hairy

It's true I still feel like an outsider here, but I'm having a *little* fun. I shoot baskets out on the driveway with the Eye-Ball. I've been practicing following up my shots—you know, running in for the rebound after I take a shot—because Mr. Donovan said it's a smart thing to do. The Eye-Ball takes funny bounces off the mountains on the backboard, but I can usually tell where it's going to go if I concentrate. I'm getting pretty good at jumping for the ball and putting the shot right back up.

And I still have fun playing with Ed. He and I like to have sock fights in the den. We roll up our socks and throw them at each other. Ed really gets a big kick out of it. I crawl around behind the couch and pop up and throw a balled-up sock at him. He throws one at me, too, and honks. I guess he's surprised at where I appear. It's sort of like a jack-in-the-box game for him. And he thinks it's a riot that I can duck out of the way of the socks he throws at me.

He's getting even better at basketball. It's true. The other guys don't have to do the behavior modification with him anymore because he's learned what to do. You can probably guess that the Lawn Ornaments are winning big.

You ought to hear Mrs. Dingley give the morning announcements. She's normal when she talks about chess club meetings and sign-up sheets for library aides and all that stuff, but she sounds absolutely bloodthirsty when she gets to the basketball results. According to her, we "chewed up" Chester Greenwood Middle School (named for the guy from Farmington, Maine, who invented earmuffs), "bombed" Baxter Bay at their place and "bashed" them at ours, and "massacred" Mussel River away and "mangled" them at home.

I think Dexter knew what he was talking about on Sheep Island that day when he said Ed is being used. It doesn't seem right to win by sixty points and gloat over it.

By the way, I'm not mad at Dexter anymore, and I apologized for saying he was just jealous of Ed.

Let's see . . . what else?

Remember the letter-jacket sweater Elizabeth knitted for me for Christmas? Kids at school thought it was geeky. Well, she gave one to Ed about a week ago, and now *everybody* wants one! She has so many orders to fill that she had to ask Mrs. Donovan to help her.

Elizabeth is a lot older than Mrs. Donovan, but they're getting along great. I hope Mrs. Donovan won't be so lonely now.

Here's an observation: I went to the second game against Mussel River, the time we "mangled" them at home, and it seemed to me that except for Dexter the Lawn Ornaments were just going through the motions and relying on Ed to win the game for them. The fans seemed listless, too.

Now here's the bad news—the line of ceramic lawn ornaments Victor designed for the Christmas season didn't do well. The thing is, Mr. Bumstock told him what to design—the same old stuff his company has sold for years and years—and now he's blaming Victor, even though Victor gave him exactly what he wanted. It's Victor's opinion that the public finally wants to put something different on their lawns. He's determined to design some winners for the spring season.

This is the weird news—on January 11, a traveling salesman caught a glimpse of two adult Bigfoots in the woods near Bangor, Maine, in the middle of the state. Because sightings of Bigfoots are still so rare, the Fish and Game people in Augusta thought the guy probably saw a couple goofball students from the University of Maine, which is near Bangor, dressed up like Bigfoots and trying to pull a nutty.

Then on January 16 a teenage girl doing her paper route early in the morning saw two adult Bigfoots on the outskirts of Ellsworth, a town on the coast north of here, and they looked like the ones the salesman said he saw, and she was close enough to them to know they were real.

When you take into account how good Bigfoots are at camouflage, you have to wonder why there have been two sightings in one month. . . .

February 1

◆

Boy, the weather is weird in Maine. A warm spell hit today, and all of us kids got spring fever a couple months early.

Evidently Mr. Gimpwater thought it was a good day for a fire drill; we had one during English. After my class lined up out back in the parking lot, I turned around to see how Ed was doing. He was gone.

I found him wandering around the woods like some guy on a TV show who's supposed to have amnesia.

At night we played Chester Greenwood and won 31 to 29. Ed was awful. He mostly just stood around acting lost while the game went on around him.

I had never seen so many empty seats in our gym.

After the game I went to Rodney's with Ed and my parents. Ed was the only Lawn Ornament who showed up for his free hamburgers, and we were the only customers there.

Rodney and I talked about what was going wrong on the island. I said, "I think basketball just isn't as much fun as it used to be."

She said, "That's what I think, too. It's funny, you'd think having a winning team would make everybody want to get together here at the café and celebrate, but I tell you, if the Lawn Ornaments keep on winning, I'm going to go out of business."

February 3

———————————●———————————

*T*onight the Lawn Ornaments played an away game at Port Alfred and lost 40 to 25. Ed was even worse than he was two nights ago. Mr. Donovan had the other Lawn Ornaments do the behavior modification to try to keep him in line, but it didn't work. When the Lawn Ornaments clapped, Ed clapped, and when they clucked, he clucked.

He fouled out early.

Even though I'm not on the team anymore, I still ride the team bus with Ed to keep him company. On our way back to the island, Mr. Donovan asked me what was wrong with Ed.

I said, "It's this warm weather—it must seem like spring to him. I bet he thinks it's time to go back home to the woods."

"Hmmm, that makes a lot of sense," said Mr. Donovan. He looked thoughtful for a minute. "But do you

84

think he can hang around until we make it into the tournament? We only have two more games."

I said, "I think so. It's too early for him to go. This warm weather's not going to last, and it's still freezing way up in the woods."

The thought of Ed leaving made me feel bad.

Mr. Donovan said, "Good," but he didn't look any happier than I felt.

February 5

———————●———————

Ed is mixed up. I'd even say depressed. He doesn't want to play with me, and his eyes are dull, and he hardly eats anything. I think he's having a hard time deciding if he wants to live like a human being or a Bigfoot.

Sundays used to be fun for us, but today was bad.

Ed nibbled one slice of bread for lunch and then he took off. I wanted to go with him, but Elizabeth said I should let him go and have some time alone.

I miss the old Ed. I wish we could have a sock fight or goof around with the volcano or even just watch "The Three Stooges" together. I wish I could cheer him up, too. I've tried, and I can't. It's frustrating.

While I hung around at home waiting for him to come back, the weather finally changed, and we were hit by a sudden cold snap.

It was getting late when Elizabeth finally gave in

and let me go look for Ed. I went straight to the area behind the kilns because I knew that was where he'd go when it got cold outside.

He wasn't there, but I saw his footprints leading into the woods, so I trailed him.

His route bothered me. He was just drifting. He'd go in one direction for a while, and then he'd go in another.

Eventually I came to a part of the woods I hadn't explored before. It was creepy listening to the wind in the trees.

Then I heard a moan.

My first thought was "That's a ghost. Run for it." But I guess I was too scared to run. When I heard the moan again, it sounded familiar. I walked toward it with my hands up—ready for anything.

It was Ed.

He was lying in a gully next to some partly frozen water—too big for a puddle, but too small for a pond. I could see a big hole in the ice where he had fallen through.

I slid down the bank and ran to him. He was all curled up in a ball and shivering like you wouldn't believe. His hair was full of tiny icicles, and his poncho was frozen stiff.

He didn't look at me or anything. He just lay there moaning and shaking. I tried to get him up, but I couldn't move him, and he didn't seem to want to move. I've got to tell you, I thought he was dying.

Finally he got up on his hands and knees, and I

knew he was going to live. Then he stood up, and I hugged him as hard as I could for a long time.

I put my coat over his head and shoulders and walked him home. Victor met us in the driveway and hustled Ed into the house. He said, "Ed, you poor thing, you're frozen. You look like a statue."

Elizabeth fixed Ed some hot cocoa and turned up the heat in his room. He went to bed and fell asleep right away, but when I looked in on him later, he was tossing and turning.

I don't know what to do about him. He's not happy here anymore. I'd never seen anybody look as miserable as he did lying out there in the woods freezing. But if we take him back where he came from, he'll be cold all the time and he won't have a house to go into to warm up.

I don't know what to do.

February 7

────────────●────────────

Ed is sick in bed, buried under a pile of blankets. When he blows his nose, the fake flowers fly around.

Now that you know Ed's sick, you can guess that the Lawn Ornaments lost tonight. They were pathetic. It was the same old story—no teamwork. Mr. Donovan is getting sick of it.

You know how a gym can get really quiet all of a sudden? Well, our game was at Muskie tonight, and during the third quarter their gym went silent for about ten seconds when Roland was running in front of the Spruce Island bench after he had hogged the ball three trips down the court in a row and missed his shot every time. He threw up his hands and said, "Do I have to do everything myself?"

Mr. Donovan yelled, "Call time!"

Roland called time out. The team gathered around Mr. Donovan. I couldn't make out much of what he was saying, but I could see he was really steamed. When the Lawn Ornaments took the floor after the time-out, Roland stayed on the bench and didn't get back in all night.

Up in the Spruce Island rooting section where I was sitting with Victor (Elizabeth was home with Ed) it sounded like the start of the season. The fans were complaining that Mr. Donovan doesn't know how to coach and why was he keeping the best player on the bench and he can't let all the boys play and expect to win and blah-blah-blah-blah-blah. I almost told them that the Lawn Ornaments could win if they'd just stop playing selfishly and do what Mr. Donovan said, but I kept my mouth shut because I can't afford to antagonize people if I want to have any hope of fitting in here sometime before I retire.

Mr. Bumstock was so mad that he left the bleachers early and paced the lobby until the end of the game. Mr. Gimpwater went out and paced behind him.

We lost 54 to 30.

Earlier in the day Victor had handed in his designs for the spring line of lawn ornaments. He didn't come right out and say it, but I could tell he thought they were just what the public wanted. He had that happy, hopeful expression on his face all through the game, and I could see he was itching to find out how Mr. Bumstock liked them.

When we got out to the lobby, he went up to Mr. Bumstock and tapped him on the shoulder. "Excuse me, Mr. Bumstock," he said, "I was wondering if you've had a chance to look at my new designs."

Mr. Bumstock whirled around. His face was bright red. "Designs?" he sputtered. "You call those designs? What are you trying to do, Dewlap? Put me out of business?"

Victor went pale. "No, I—"

"They're a disgrace to the proud name of Bumstock! I don't even know what they're supposed to be! What's that lumpy green monstrosity?"

"I call it 'Renewal.' "

"I call it junk! And the white blob with the pink streaks? That one looks like a pile of fish guts! Do you think the homeowners of America want to put statues of fish guts on their front lawns?"

"It's not supposed to look like fish guts—"

"Well, it does!"

Victor took a moment to compose himself. He said, "It's nonrepresentational. I intended it to express the miracle of springtime, and I think people would—"

"People would laugh at me! That's what they'd do! And you'd like that, wouldn't you, Dewlap? Well, I'm not going to give you the chance to make a monkey out of me—*you're fired!* Do you hear me? Fired! Get your things out of my factory tomorrow and go fry your eye!"

February 8

───────●───────

*V*ictor came in the kitchen door and put his stuff from work on the table. He said, "From now on, Victor Dewlap works on his own. I don't need Ludlow Bumstock to tell me what to do."

Elizabeth said, "Of course not, clam cake. He doesn't understand art, and he doesn't understand you at all."

I said, "I guess the Dewlaps don't fit in here any better than Ed does. We're just different."

Victor said, "You're right, we *are* different—but that's why we fit in."

"Huh?"

"We all have to find our niche—our own place in the world and our special way to live our lives. If you try to fit in by being just like somebody else, you'll never make it, because there's already somebody else filling that niche."

I needed a minute to think. Victor raised his eyebrows and watched me. "I get it," I said. "If we were all alike, *nobody* would fit in."

Victor said, "Exactly. It's like basketball. When all of the players do what they're supposed to do, the team plays beautifully. But when they forget their own assignments and try to do something they're not supposed to do, the team loses."

Elizabeth said, "My honeybunch is a basketball genius!"

February 10

———●———

*E*d feels better. It seems to me his emotional state is improving, too; he seems less mixed up. I think the cold weather we've been having the past few days has helped him decide to stay here on the island until spring comes for real. He's been hanging around in the little ceramics studio in our cellar, probably napping next to the kiln, while Victor works on a secret lawn ornament project.

I wish Ed could tell me what Victor is making. . . .

I was eating a bowl of Bran Man cereal this morning when Mr. Donovan knocked on the kitchen door. He said he wanted to give Ed and me a ride to school. I told him Ed was getting better, but I wasn't sure he felt up to going back to school yet.

Mr. Donovan said, "He has to. If he doesn't go to school today, he can't play basketball tonight—and we need him."

He explained that Rockweed Harbor—our opponent tonight—had a record of 10–2 and would make
it into the tournament for sure along with Edmund S.
Muskie, who had ended the regular season at 11–2,
and Port Alfred, who finished up at 9–4. "Right now,"
he said, "our record is seven and five. If we lose tonight, we'll be tied with Potato Head at seven and six
for the fourth spot in the tournament. And there are
only four spots."

"What happens if we finish tied? Do we both get
into the tournament?" I asked.

"No. Only four teams get in. And if we end up tied,
Potato Head gets in because they won the only game
we played against them this season." That was the
game we forfeited because we suited up thirteen players. Remember?

"I see. So if we lose tonight, we're finished."

"Right," said Mr. Donovan. "And if the Lawn Ornaments are finished, I'm finished."

I woke Ed up and got him ready for school. When
we were in the van, Mr. Donovan said, "I'll take it
easy on him, okay? If I can get away with leaving him
on the bench all night, I'll do it. It's just that I have
to win this game. You know. Once we make it into
the tournament, the pressure will be off. But we have
to make it into the tournament."

A big crowd turned out for the game tonight. Some
of the islanders who had stopped going to the games
went to this one. There weren't many Rockweedians

there because the game didn't mean much to them—
they were in the tournament whether they won or lost.

But even though the game didn't mean much to the
Rockweed Harbor fans, it was really important to the
Rockweed Harbor coach. He was all riled up. I bet
he'd been stewing about this whole Bigfoot issue ever
since the rules committee said Ed could play. He was
chewing five sticks of gum at a time.

Ed stayed on the bench the whole first half. At first
the Lawn Ornaments didn't look too bad—even the
reserves did okay—but in the second quarter, Roland
reverted to his selfish ways and hogged the ball and
played out of position and ruined Mr. Donovan's
game plan. When he went bad, the others did, too,
except Dexter, who really ought to be given the Rud-
yard Kipling Award for keeping his head when all
about him are losing theirs.

At halftime the Fightin' Clams were up by ten
points, and I could see Mr. Bumstock fuming. Boy,
you'd think the world was going to end if the Lawn
Ornaments got shut out of the tournament.

Roland hardly played at all in the third quarter, and
Ed stayed on the bench. At the end of the quarter,
Rockweed Harbor had a fourteen-point lead.

I heard Mr. Bumstock say, "Why bother to play at
all? Donovan's just *giving* the game to Rockweed Harbor. I've never seen anything like it. And he's doing
this just to get at me, you know. Why else would he
play a bunch of uncoordinated ninnies and leave the
big gorilla on the bench? That Ed Tibbetts is the best

ballplayer this island has seen since the year ol' Doc Thompson's team won the State Class D title! Island boys—"

He went on, but I didn't listen. I was wondering how he could confuse a Bigfoot with a gorilla, and I was also wondering how the parents sitting near him liked hearing him call their sons "uncoordinated ninnies."

Mr. Donovan was nervous. He was sweating through his jacket. Ugh.

When the fourth quarter started, Spruce Island's five best players were on the court, and they included Roland, Dexter, and Ed. On their first trip down the court, Roland threw an alley-oop to Ed, and Ed slammed it through the hoop.

The crowd went crazy—and so did the Rockweed coach. He got purple in the face, and the veins on his forehead stuck out. He was so mad to see Ed in the game that he ripped off his plaid sport coat, threw it on the floor, and stomped on it (and believe me, any jacket *that* ugly deserves to be stomped on).

Ed kept on blocking the Fightin' Clams' shots when they had the ball and scoring at will when we had it. The Rockweed coach called time out. I can't testify under oath as to what he told his players, but when they got back out on the floor, they played rough. They elbowed Ed in the back and kicked him in the ankles and got away with it because they stayed behind him, where the officials couldn't see them.

The strategy worked. All that nasty stuff distracted

Ed enough to make him blow a couple of easy shots and play out of position once in a while on defense. But the strategy also got Dexter mad, and he played better than ever. He was really, really aggressive under the boards, and when he played defense, he shut down everything on his section of the court.

As a result, the Lawn Ornaments won 42 to 39 and finished the regular season with a record of 8–5. They got into the tournament, and now Mr. Donovan can keep his job.

When I was standing down by the bench after the final buzzer had sounded, I heard Mr. Bumstock say to Mr. Donovan, "You did the right thing. I'm proud of you."

Mr. Donovan walked away without saying a word.

February 14

———————●———————

*T*he mailman had to ring our doorbell because he had so many valentines for our house that he couldn't fit all of them in our mailbox. There were 177 of them! There was one for Victor and Elizabeth from me, one for Victor from Elizabeth, one for Elizabeth from Victor, one for me from Victor and Elizabeth, and 173 for Ed. He got them from all over the country. I guess stories about him are still popping up in newspapers from time to time.

There was a Valentine's Day dance at school tonight. I wasn't going to go, but a lot of kids asked me if I'd take Ed, and I said I would. (He's still not as happy as he was when we met on Christmas, but he's feeling much better than he was during that stupid midwinter thaw, and he's not stumbling along in a personal fog anymore, so I figured it would be okay to take him.)

It was a magical event, a night to remember. (It's hard to make yourself sound sarcastic in print. I'm trying. Picture me rolling my eyes and smirking.)

The dance was held in the cafeteria because street shoes aren't allowed on the gym floor, and if you let kids dance in their socks, they end up running around and sliding on the floor. If they wear shoes, they just run around. I know. I've been there.

As you might expect, the smell of deodorant and pimple cream was overpowering.

The first kids to dance were the cheerleaders. They made a circle and did a dance that looked like a cheering routine—you know, shuffling around and making lots of hand gestures. Come to think of it, that's pretty much how they walk down the halls in school, too—clapping silently and slapping their thighs and making judo-chop motions.

One of them came over to me. For one horrifying instant I thought she was going to drag me out there, but she wanted Ed. He joined her and the other cheerleaders and had a great time. My grandmother would say, "He has a lovely sense of rhythm."

After a few more fast songs, the disc jockey played a slow one and got that ridiculous mirrored ball going. Let me tell you, I was enchanted. (Smirk.) Apparently none of the girls felt like slow-dancing with Ed. He came back and stood against the wall with Dexter and me.

We watched the other kids dance. It was a pathetic sight, sort of a three-minute nap with boys and girls draped over each other, moving as little as possible, and sweating profusely. There was a general feeling of release when the song ended and the couples pried themselves apart.

Roland LeMay was walking around the perimeter of the room as slowly as he could, allowing everybody to get a good look at him. I think he had taken a pencil to his fabulous manly mustache. What a cement-head.

When another slow song started, he came over to us, stood in front of a girl I don't know, made this incredibly masculine face, and said, "Dance." It wasn't a request; it was a command. She laughed at him.

He grabbed her by the wrist and started to lead her onto the dance floor. She made a nice escape—I think she must watch wrestling on TV—and walked back to the wall.

Roland said, "Come on. Dance."

She said, "No."

Roland said, "Why not?"

She said, "Because you make me sick."

I laughed. I shouldn't have. Even though I can't stand Roland, I didn't want to make an official enemy of him.

But I couldn't help it.

He grabbed me by the shirt and said, "Outside. You and me. Right now. Let's settle this."

I said, "Go out by yourself. I'm not going to fight you."

"Chicken?"

"Or course," I said.

I think that answer surprised him. He said, "I'm going to murderlize you one of these days, Dewlap." Then he took off.

I was feeling pretty brave because I was with Dexter, and I knew Roland wouldn't try anything with chaperons all over the place, but I was a little scared just the same.

Ed went back out on the dance floor and did the cheering routines just as well as the cheerleaders. I was waiting for Dexter to say something about my run-in with Roland, but I would have had to wait forever. He minds his own business.

Finally I brought up the topic. I asked him how he thought I had handled the situation, and he said he didn't know. I asked him if he thought Roland was going to pound me into a pile of hamburger, and he said he didn't know. I was hoping he'd say, "Don't worry about Roland. I'll take care of him." Instead he said, "You've got to fight your own battles."

I said, "But I don't want to fight anybody. I don't need enemies—I need friends. Remember?"

Dexter said, "Why do you want a guy like that for a friend?"

I didn't have an answer at the time, but now that I've had a couple hours to think, I've decided it's because I want *everyone* to like me. I don't know if that's good or bad. It's probably pretty unrealistic.

Okay, maybe Roland will never be my friend. I can accept that. I just hope he won't be my executioner.

February 15

───────────●───────────

*T*he Down East League tournament will start on Friday, February 17. We're seeded fourth, so we play Rockweed Harbor, the top seed. The other game that night is number two Muskie against number three Port Alfred. The two winners meet on Saturday night for the championship game.

They always hold the tournament at Spruce Island because we have the biggest and nicest gym. It's true the Lawn Ornaments get the home-court advantage, but our gym holds lots more people than the other schools' gyms, so nobody beefs about it too much— except the Rockweed Harbor coach. If he had his way, his team would play all its games at home and he'd referee.

The tournament is shaping up to be an even bigger deal than I'd expected. Adults are going cuckoo about it. There was a story in the paper about a typical day in the life of a Port Alfred player: what time he gets up, what he eats for breakfast, what subjects he takes, what time he goes to bed—everything. Another piece was about the personal lives of the Muskie guys, like which ones like ice fishing and which ones collect baseball cards—hot stuff like that. It seems odd to me that the prestige of four communities depends on the ability of a bunch of kids to put a ball in a basket.

When I was thinking about all this stuff, the phone rang. It was Mr. Donovan.

He told me a secret and asked me not to tell anybody.

February 16

When Ed and I arrived at school this morning, kids were hanging up posters that said stuff like "Go, Lawn Ornaments" and "We're Number One." We really aren't number one—we're number four. And if I hadn't promised Mr. Donovan not to tell the secret he told me, I could have explained to everybody why I thought we'd stay number four.

It wasn't easy keeping my mouth shut all day when all the kids were talking about the tournament and how great we were going to do and everything, but I did, because I knew it wouldn't be long until practice—and then the guys on the team would know, too, and once they knew, everyone would know.

The bell finally rang at two-thirty, and Ed and I walked to the locker room. Mr. Donovan usually stays in the coaches' room until practice starts, but today he was standing by the lockers. When all the players had arrived, he started his talk.

He said, "Boys, we face a big challenge tomorrow night; Rockweed Harbor is a good team. But I think we're better."

O. said, "We're the greatest."

Right.

Mr. Donovan went on. "We're all going to have to play to the best of our ability if we're going to win. And that means playing as a team. Each man has to do his job." He took a breath and rubbed his beard. "And there's one more thing. We're going to have to win it without Ed."

I looked around at the guys. Only Dexter had maintained his composure. The others were making the face that little kids make when their baby-sitters tell them it's time for bed.

Mr. Donovan said, "I took advantage of Ed to save my job, even though I thought using him was unfair. I'm not proud of what I did, but I *am* proud to say that as of right now, Ed Tibbetts is off the team." He looked at me. "And, Picasso, you can get back on if you'd like to."

I took a quick glance at Roland. He squinted at me, made a fist, and shook his head just a little so only I could see.

I declined Mr. Donovan's offer.

Most of the guys were beefing about how it wasn't fair and how did he expect them to beat anybody and all that stuff when Mr. Donovan held up his hands and said, "If we win, we're going to win with boys—

human boys. You can do it. You can win. Now let's have a good practice."

We had a terrible practice.

When it was over, Mr. Donovan said, "I'm ashamed of this team. You think you've already lost. Well, if you think you have, you have. Now get out of here, and come back tomorrow with a better attitude."

Boy, was there ever a sour mood in the locker room. You'd think all the guys were on death row—except Dexter. He just showered and got dressed and kept to himself. Roland dragged out his old speech about how Mr. Donovan doesn't know how to coach. And the more Roland beefed, the madder he got.

When he was at his angriest, he came over to me. I knew something was up. He said, "You want us to lose, don't you? That's why you told Donovan Ed can't play."

He shoved me against the tiled wall. I had never fought anybody before, and I didn't want to start, but it was looking as if I didn't have any choice.

Roland said, "You're just jealous of me because you know I'm the greatest player we have, and the only way you can get back at me is to make sure we lose. That's why you told Donovan that Ed can't play anymore. You want us to lose, don't you?"

He shoved me again. A crowd was gathering. I was hoping Dexter would jump in, but he didn't.

I said, "No, I don't."

Roland said, "You want us all to be losers like you and your stupid loser can't-hold-a-job *father!*"

I'd been scared for a while. Now I was scared and *mad.* All of a sudden it didn't matter what Roland thought of me. I was going to tell him what I really thought of him and take the consequences.

I said, "I'm not a loser, and my father's not a loser. *You're* the loser, Roland. *You're* making the team lose. If you'd stop hogging the ball and showing off and start doing what Mr. Donovan says, you guys could win—"

He shoved me again, and I put up my fists to defend myself. That was the signal for Roland to throw a punch.

He threw a right at my head. I was extra alert because my life and my million-dollar face were in jeopardy, so it was no trouble to see his fist coming. It was easier than ducking the balled-up socks Ed throws at me. I simply lowered my head and heard Roland's knuckles hit the wall behind me. Some bones in his hand crumpled.

The whole "fight" was over in two seconds. I wasn't touched, and Roland had a broken hand.

He cried like a baby.

After supper Mr. Donovan dropped by our house. He asked me if I would reconsider and join the team. Now that I'd stood up to Roland and stopped letting him scare me, I thought playing with the Lawn Ornaments sounded like a good idea.

I thought about it for three nanoseconds and said yes.

February 17

———————●———————

A reporter and a photographer from the *Rocky Coast Blabber* were at school all day to do a feature article called "Game Day on Spruce Island." It was easy for them to pick out us Lawn Ornaments from the other students because we were wearing jackets and ties for the last-period rally.

It could have been just my imagination, but it seemed to me the other kids looked at me a little differently today when I passed them in the halls between classes. I don't think it was the jacket and tie, either; I think they thought it was good that I had stood up to Roland.

Everybody was in a good mood. Even Dexter got a little goofy. At lunch he sucked up his Jell-O through a straw.

Usually at rallies the players sit on the stage and look as serious as they can, but today we all had a good time. Ed did a couple of numbers with the cheer-leaders, and even Mr. Donovan got up and tried to dance with them a little. He wasn't as good as Ed.

You know what? I think one of the reasons Ed likes cheering so much is all the clapping. I think he associ-ates it with his basketball training. And now that he's clapping along with everybody, he probably thinks ev-erything is going just great for everybody—and I guess it is.

Our game against Rockweed Harbor was the first half of the tournament doubleheader. Port Alfred against Edmund S. Muskie was the second. I got to school early and had to wait outdoors by the side of the gym for Mr. Donovan to open the locker room door for us. My feet were getting cold, so I walked around the corner to see if he had shown up yet. I saw about two hundred of our fans from the island milling around on the steps that lead up to the gym doors, all talking about the tournament. That much hot breath smacking into the cold air made a good-size vapor cloud form over their heads.

Then I saw Mr. and Mrs. Donovan walking up the concrete path to the front of the gym. The islanders gave them a big round of applause.

I heard a *BLAT!*

It was Victor, up by the gym doors, standing on the pedestal that supports the flagpole. He put his boat horn back into his coat pocket.

"Attention, please," he said. "I have something to present to Coach Donovan on behalf of the residents of Spruce Island as a token of thanks for all the enjoyment he's provided for us and our children this winter. Whether we win or lose tonight, we've all had a good season, and we've been lucky to have the Donovans living among us."

The islanders' blank looks told me they didn't know what was going on—even though Victor said he was acting on their behalf—but, confused as they were, they clapped.

Mr. Donovan walked up the steps, and Victor got down from the pedestal. He picked up something about three feet tall that was wrapped in brown paper and handed it to Mr. Donovan. Mr. Donovan ripped it open, revealing a ceramic lawn ornament. It was a statue of Ed, one foot on the ground, taking a hook shot, and it was beautiful!

Evidently Ed had been *posing*, not napping, in Victor's studio.

Mrs. Donovan cried a little because she was so happy. Mr. Donovan shook Victor's hand and looked at all the islanders gathered around him. He said, "This is wonderful. I've never seen a nicer piece of ceramic lawn ornament art. How can I thank you all?"

A voice from the back of the crowd said, *"Win."*

It was Mr. Bumstock. The islanders cleared a path for him. He walked up to Mr. Donovan and said, "Win tonight and win tomorrow night—or you're fired."

Mr. Donovan looked surprised. He said, "But you told me I could keep my job if we made it into the tournament. And here we are. You can't go back on your word now."

"Don't tell me what I can and can't do. I won't take orders from any goon who's too stupid to use an eight-foot-tall player."

Mr. Donovan's face got all hard looking. He said, "*Use* is the right word for it. We've been using an animal unfairly against children just to satisfy a selfish old man who thinks he's the king of the world. Well, no more, Bumstock. We're going to play without Ed tonight because it's not fair to use him. The Rockweed Harbor coach was right. And if we lose, well, that's better than cheating to win."

The islanders applauded.

Mr. Bumstock glared at some of them individually and said, "I won't forget this."

Then he left.

The photographer took a lot of pictures of the Ed lawn ornament, and the reporter was taking notes as fast as he could.

When I got out on the gym floor with the team for warm-ups, the pep band was playing and Ed was dancing with the cheerleaders and the bleachers were jammed and I felt just as excited as I did for my first game in December.

I played a few minutes in both of the first two quarters and didn't do too badly. I think all the practicing in our driveway is paying off.

Near the end of the first half, when Dexter and O.

were both on the bench, the Fightin' Clams got a few offensive rebounds and put them back up for easy baskets. At the end of the half, we were down by five points.

During halftime Mr. Donovan said we were doing a good job, and if we'd just keep it up, we'd be fine.

In the first minute of the second half, O. caught an elbow under the eye. A mouse developed immediately. This was what he'd been afraid of all along— playing under the basket and getting hammered. Mr. Donovan went out to look at him.

O. said, "It's nothing. Let's play."

We were shocked. The thing is, after O. got hurt, he played better. He wasn't afraid to rebound anymore. And before long, we had caught up.

I played a few minutes and got two baskets by following my shots. I could tell where the ball was going to go when it bounced off the rim, so I just went there and jumped and grabbed the ball and put it right back up—twice.

The Rockweed coach was going nuts. He called a time-out and screamed at his players. He yanked one of them right off the court and shook him by the shoulders. Some of the Rockweed Harbor fans booed when they saw that.

He must have said what he said the last time we played Rockweed. When the players took the floor, they started playing dirty, doing the things they did to Ed in the other game, but this time they were doing the dirty stuff to kids their own size, not to Ed, so the officials got a good look at what they were doing and started blowing their whistles.

We kept going to the foul line and making our free throws. After a while the Fightin' Clams stopped playing that way—I don't think they wanted to in the first place—but their coach kept yelling at them to get tough. The Rockweed fans booed him until he shut up.

With a minute left in the game, Mr. Donovan took Dexter out for the last time. The crowd gave him a standing ovation. I guess without Ed and that show-off Roland on the court, they had a chance to see what a good player Dexter really is. I'm glad Dexter got recognized. He responded to the ovation by putting on his warm-ups, drinking some water, and staring down at the floor.

We won 48 to 33.

February 18

———————●———————

When I went downstairs for breakfast, the sun was already bouncing off the seven inches of snow that had fallen during the night, and the kitchen was filled with bright sunlight. I opened the *Rocky Coast Blabber* and read while I ate.

The sports section was full of stories about last night's games: how we had "upended" Rockweed Harbor and Muskie had "turned back" Port Alfred. The features section ran the story about game day on Spruce Island. I looked particularly debonair in one picture, wearing my jacket and tie at lunch in the cafeteria. (Come to think of it, it's not too hard to look debonair when the guy sitting next to you in the picture is eating his Jell-O through a straw.)

I guess the picture of Victor giving the Ed statue to Mr. Donovan got on the wire services to some of the big city papers, because in the middle of the morning

Victor got a few calls from art galleries in Portland and Boston and New York, and a couple of people asked if they could be exclusive distributors of his lawn ornaments.

Victor is rocking the ceramics world!

I was nervous. I tried watching the Saturday morning cartoons on TV and reading a comic book and shooting elastics and setting up army men with Ed and knocking them over with a tennis ball, but nothing I did took my mind off the championship game.

Then the phone rang, and it was for me. A deep, muffled voice said, "Don't play in the game tonight if you know what's good for you."

For a second I was scared, but then I wondered who would care if I played in the game—it wasn't as if I were some kind of all-American or anything.

The voice said, "If you play, Dewlap, I'll murderlize you."

That was all I had to hear. I said, "Does your mother know you make crank calls, Roland?"

"Huh? Don't tell! Um, wait a minute! This isn't Roland LeMay. This is somebody else, and I'm real big—"

I was laughing too hard to talk, so I hung up. If Roland meant to spoil my day and keep me from playing, he failed. In fact, he was so ridiculous that I loosened up and stayed relaxed until it was time to go to the game.

At six-thirty Ed and I left the house and walked along the plowed road toward the school; moonlight was shining on the snow now instead of sunlight. After we passed the softball field and the skating pond, we entered the village and saw green and white pennants attached to the orange ceramic basketballs on top of the lampposts.

I thought about Roland as we went by his house, and I felt sorry for a kid who was so mixed up in the head that he had to show off all the time and bully people in order to feel good. Maybe he'll smarten up someday. I hope so.

At the edge of the village we left the road and took a shortcut on a trail that runs through a field and some woods. Right in the middle of the field were two enormous snowmen standing side by side. They must have been ten or eleven feet tall. I made a snowball and threw it at one of them.

The snowman caught it.

Instantly the snowmen blew apart, and two adult Bigfoots, a female and a male, came out of them like dinosaurs hatching from eggs, but faster—*much* faster! They ran straight at us, and before we could even move, they grabbed us and covered our mouths with their giant hairy hands so we couldn't yell for help.

The female hustled Ed into the woods on foot. The male picked me up and carried me on his hip right behind the female and Ed. His hair was long and silky, but the areas of his body I bumped against while he ran with me were hard and muscular. He smelled like a dog.

As you can probably imagine, I was *terrified.*

When we came to a clearing in the woods, we stopped. The male put me down but continued to hold me with one hand and keep the other over my mouth. Some of his hairs tickled my nose.

I looked at Ed. He had his arms wrapped around the female, and she was rubbing his head. They were mumbling like Popeye and making a purring sound. I didn't have to be a genius to figure out that Ed had been reunited with his mother.

The Bigfoots that were spotted near Bangor and Ellsworth must have been these two, and the only thing that could have made them reckless enough to forget to camouflage themselves would be their desperation to get their boy back.

After a moment Ed's mother took control of me, and Ed got to hug his father. They muttered and purred, and then Ed's father plucked at the Ed Sweater that Ed had on and uttered a quiet honk. Ed honked, too, and they both covered their mouths like people laughing in church.

Then Ed's mother picked me up, and all four of us headed off through the woods for the shoreline. We came out on a tiny pebbly beach. Ed's father uncovered a dinghy hidden under some snow-covered pine boughs and dragged it to the water.

We got in. I sat in the stern with Ed's father, who still had one hand over my mouth. (It actually covered most of my face.)

Ed muttered something to his mother. When she smiled and nodded her head, he clapped his hands and then picked up the oars and started to row. We were headed for the mainland. I could see the headlights of a line of cars carrying Muskie fans across the crib-stone bridge far off to the left.

I wondered what they planned to do with me. Maybe they were taking me with them just until they'd made their getaway, and then they'd let me go. But maybe Ed had asked them if they would take me all the way up to Sasquatch country. The situation looked bad. I knew I wouldn't last long in the wild. Then again, maybe I wouldn't even make it out of the county. Maybe the police would arrest Ed's parents for kidnapping me and throw them in prison.

Or maybe the police would shoot them. That would be awful.

I didn't know what to do. Then one or two of the long hairs on Ed's father's wrist tickled the inside of my nose. I sneezed. I guess the sneeze felt funny on his palm or surprised him or something, because he pulled his hand away from my face. In that one moment I made up my mind to make a break for it. I did a backward somersault off the stern into the water and swam for shore.

Maybe I should say my *plan* was to swim for shore. The water was wicked cold. I couldn't take a breath, and I couldn't move my arms or legs. My clothes felt as if they were made of rocks, and I began to sink.

Then I felt one huge, strong hand on my leg and another on my chest, and Ed's father was lifting me out of the water. When I was back in the dinghy, he and Ed's mother sandwiched me between them and rubbed me to warm me up, but I was too cold to warm up. My body shook uncontrollably, and I thought my brain might have frozen. I was numb. Ed took off his Ed Sweater and passed it to his father. His father slipped it over my head and pulled it down over my wet clothes.

It didn't do any good.

I thought I was going to die. I really did. I thought I was going to catch pneumonia and die in the wilderness and never see my parents again. And when I thought about that, I cried. Ed's mother leaned close and made soothing sounds in my ear, but I kept crying and put my hands over my face so Ed wouldn't see.

While I had my hands over my face, the movement of the dinghy began to feel different. The wind was hitting me at a different angle, too, and I could hear Ed and his parents talking to one another. Something was up.

I dropped my hands from my face and saw we had reversed direction. I guess Ed *had* seen me crying, and he was rowing us back to Spruce Island!

Before long Mr. Donovan was holding the locker room door open for me and I was walking out of the cold into the warmth. "What happened?" he said.

I wasn't able to answer right away because I didn't have much control over my face; I couldn't get my mouth to form words. Before I said anything, Mr.

Donovan noticed Ed outside and said, "Come in, Ed, come in."

While I was rubbing my face and getting a little blood circulating, Ed, who was still outside, looked away from Mr. Donovan and muttered something in the direction of some pine trees. A few seconds later Mr. Donovan backpedaled into the locker room with his jaw hanging open.

Ed came in, and then his parents followed him, ducking to fit through the doorway. The Lawn Ornaments gathered around and stared at Ed's parents, but none of them made a sound. When I was sure my mouth was going to work, I said, "Mr. Donovan, Lawn Ornaments, meet Mr. and Mrs. Tibbetts."

In the next ten minutes or so, I dried off and got my temperature up pretty close to normal. I gave Ed back his Ed Sweater, and Dexter dried it for him with his hair dryer. Mr. and Mrs. Tibbetts stayed in the coaches' room until it was time for us to go out on the floor. They must have been apprehensive about being around people, but Ed mumbled to them for a while and apparently assured them that nobody in the gym would hurt them.

When we—including the Tibbetts family—took the floor, some fans scrambled out of the bleachers and ran for the exits. That was understandable. Mr. Tibbetts stood ten feet tall—as high as a basket—and Mrs. Tibbetts was a foot taller.

Victor and Elizabeth left their seats and introduced themselves to Mr. and Mrs. Tibbetts, and Ed evidently told his parents that my parents were okay. The four of them climbed to the top row of the bleachers and sat together.

Ed joined the cheerleaders and did the "Spruce Island Spell-Out" with them, twisting himself and sticking out his arms and legs to form all the letters. I looked up in the bleachers and saw that his parents were delighted to see how talented he was.

The pep bands from both schools played the national anthem together. It's too bad they couldn't agree on a key, but everybody stood at attention and looked at the flag and sang anyway.

As soon as the singing stopped, the chanting began on both sides of the court, kids and grown-ups all yelling along with the two schools' cheerleaders. I'd never heard so much noise before.

I felt hot and cold.

That's when it hit me: *We were playing for the Down East League championship.*

Gulp.

And get this—two of our guys had come down with the flu in the afternoon and were home sick in bed. We only had nine players available for the game. I'd figured the team wouldn't need me when the game was on the line, but now, with only nine players, I wasn't so sure. . . .

O. O'Malley controlled the opening tip, and the game was under way. With every trip we made up and down the court, the crowd noise grew louder and louder. We were rattled. If we could have calmed down a little, we would have done a lot better. After two minutes had gone by, we hadn't come close to making a basket—but neither had the Muskie Senators. Mr. Donovan called a time-out to settle us down.

He said, "Boys, just remember how you showed Ed how to play. Execute the fundamentals. Do your jobs. And have fun—basketball's a game."

We did better. I got in for a few minutes and didn't do anything horrible.

Dexter and O. were great. They pulled down lots of rebounds—and there were lots to pull down because both teams were cold.

The half ended with the score Spruce Island 13, Muskie 9.

While we were in the locker room eating orange sections and drinking water, the flu hit one of our reserves hard and he threw up all over the place. When he was done, Mr. Donovan helped him get into his street clothes and took him upstairs to his parents.

Now there were only eight of us left.

In the third quarter, both teams—especially us— bore down hard on defense, and the play got a little rough. The officials called things pretty tight to keep the players in line, and that was good. What was bad was that some of our guys were picking up too many fouls, even the subs.

O. kept pushing his hair out of his eyes and grunting. I'd never seen him play so hard before. He was like a tall, skinny Dexter.

One offensive highlight I have to mention is a basket I made on a little bank shot that would have bounced off the Teton Range on my backboard at home.

At the end of the third quarter we were up 19 to 13 and we were still playing as a team and looking pretty good.

I started the fourth quarter, but thank goodness I wasn't in long. There was no way I wanted to be out there at the end of the game.

Midway through the fourth quarter we got in serious foul trouble. O. got a little carried away with his aggressive play and picked up his fifth foul, He had to leave the game.

We were down to seven players.

I could see Mr. Donovan thinking about who should go in. I sat back on the bench and didn't breathe and hoped he wouldn't notice me.

He noticed me.

He didn't come right out and ask me if I wanted to go in, he just sort of looked at me and asked me without saying any words. Evidently it was pretty obvious that I wanted to stay put, so he sent the other guy in.

Mr. Donovan is an understanding coach.

The Senators started setting some screens for their best shooter, and he started hitting. With a minute to go, the score was tied at 26.

The last minute was torture. We turned the ball over, and so did the Senators. People in the stands were hollering themselves hoarse and wringing their

hands, and the guys on the court were running around
and trying to do eight things at once, and the time ran
out with the score tied at 26.

The game heated up even more in overtime. Fans
from both schools were on their feet, stomping their
boots on the bleachers. The rumble sounded like an
earthquake. It even drowned out the cheerleaders.

Dexter got four points, and Muskie got four points,
and we went into double overtime tied at 30.

Nobody scored in the second overtime period. I
guess you could say everybody choked, but we're only
kids, so what do you want? The important thing was
I was still on the bench.

But I was sweating gumdrops because another one
of our guys had fouled out. We were down to six
players, and two of our remaining guys had four fouls.
I crossed all my fingers and I tried to cross my toes,
but there wasn't enough room in my sneakers, so I
crossed my feet—all in the hope that I wouldn't have
to play and do something stupid and lose the game
for us and undo all the progress I had made in fitting
in here on the island.

Right after the third overtime started, there was a
scramble for a loose ball, and my heart stopped because I heard a whistle.

A foul was called on one of our guys. It was his
fifth.

I had to go in.

I got up and took off my warm-ups. Mr. Donovan
stood in front of me, put his hands on my shoulders,

and looked down at me with a very serious expression on his face. He said, "Hibby hibby gogo."

We both cracked up.

As I ran out onto the court, I thought of Christmas Day when Ed slid off Mr. Donovan's roof and I said, "Hibby hibby gogo." I thought of all the fun I've had with Ed, and all of a sudden I was happy to be in the game. I knew I could make something good happen. I remembered all the good things I've done this winter, like giving Ed a place to live and making friends with Dexter and quitting the team so Ed could play and speaking up at the hearing and I began to think of playing at the end of a game as another opportunity to make something good happen instead of some kind of deadly trial by fire.

Don't get the wrong idea—I did all that thinking in the time it took me to swallow hard twice. I was ready to play, and I had my mind on the game.

Muskie got a three-point lead. We took a couple of good shots, but they didn't go in. With about a minute to go, Dexter set a nice pick for me. I dribbled around him, and the man who was covering me bumped into him. For an instant, the guy covering Dexter and the guy covering me didn't know if they should switch men or not. In that instant Dexter rolled to the basket. I threw him a bounce pass, and he made the layup.

We were behind by one.

The Senators brought the ball up the court against us, panicked, and threw it out of bounds.

Then we did the same thing.

It was looking as if neither team wanted to score, and that was great for Muskie because they were in the lead.

They had a good chance for a basket, but Dexter jumped up higher than I'd ever seen him and blocked the shot. I picked up the loose ball.

Ten seconds were left on the clock, and we were down by one point. A basket would win it for us. I passed the ball to our other guard and ran down the court. Now only seven seconds were left. Two Muskie guys trapped our guy with the ball, so I ran toward him and yelled. He saw me and got the ball to me. I looked for Dexter under the basket. There was somebody on him.

I dribbled toward the foul line, hoping to see one of our guys open, but it seemed the Muskie defenders were everywhere—and there was one right in my face.

I went up for the shot.

I felt good. I had a clear view of the rim, and the ball felt good in my hands, but as I released it, the man covering me hit my forearm and fell into me.

The shot missed, but I went to the line for two free throws. If I could make one, we'd tie and go into quadruple overtime. If I made two, we'd win the Down East League championship. If I missed both shots—well, I didn't want to think about that.

Players lined up on both sides of the lane, and the referee handed me the ball. There was no noise at all from the stands. I dribbled the ball twice, and the sound rang through the gym.

As soon as I released the ball, I knew it was going to be short. I hopped around behind the line and hunched my shoulders, but once it had left my hand I couldn't do anything else to make it go in—and it didn't.

From our bench, O. said, "That's okay, Picasso! Make this one, baby! You can do it!"

Then a neat thing happened—the islanders cheered for me. They weren't mad that I had missed the first shot, they were just encouraging me to make the second one.

I relaxed and put it up, making sure to give it a little more gas than I had the first time.

I gave it too much.

The ball hit the back of the rim and bounced back toward me. I went after it. I knew exactly where it was going to go. It was just out of the reach of the two big Muskie guys and Dexter. There must have been about three seconds left on the clock when I felt the ball in my hands. I landed and jumped again as fast as I could and put it back up. It hit the backboard, bounced once on the left side of the rim, and fell off.

The guys in front of me had jumped for it too soon, but once again, because I was concentrating so hard, I had a good idea where the ball was going. I jumped.

I knew I wouldn't have time to come down with the ball and gather myself for another jump. I had to tap it in.

I did.

As the ball nestled into the net, the buzzer went off, and we had won 34 to 33.

I think I must have been too happy and excited to know I was happy and excited. All I know is that Ed picked me up and ran around the court holding me high over his head. He was honking as loud as he could, and that's pretty loud. I didn't want to be a show-off, so I worked my way down to his shoulders and then jumped to the floor. I shook his hand and then hugged him.

Then I shook with all of our guys and the Muskie players, too. Nobody had any hard feelings at all. I overheard some grown-ups saying it was too bad one of the teams had to lose, because all the boys had played so hard.

We cut down the nets from both baskets, and then the gold basketball that goes to the champions was presented to Mr. Donovan. Dexter got the tournament's Most Valuable Player award.

After the ceremonies, the Lawn Ornaments and the islanders went to Rodney's. Dexter set his trophy on the floor next to his stool while he ate his hamburgers. O. showed people the mouse under his eye and got lots of sympathy. (It was turning weird colors.) Everything was perfect. I didn't even mind when Victor and Elizabeth hugged me from both sides and almost smothered me. It wasn't a night for being embarrassed about feeling good.

Ed was teaching his parents the basics of cheerleading when all of a sudden his eyes bugged out and he pointed at the window. I looked where he was pointing and saw Mr. Bumstock's face pressed up against the glass. I felt kind of sorry for him, seeing him stuck out there in the cold watching everybody have fun inside, so I went out.

I think I startled him. He said, "What do you want, Dewlap—er, Picasso?"

I was surprised he knew my name.

"I just want to invite you in for the party."

He peered at me. I think he was trying to figure out if I was playing a trick on him, so I made sure to look right back at him and not blink. Then he said, "Do you think they want an old geezer like me in there? I didn't even go to the game."

I said, "All the more reason to go in now and talk about it."

He walked with me. When we got inside, he cleared his throat until the people gave him their attention. "I have an announcement to make," he said in a loud voice. "Ludlow Bumstock is a nincompoop. I want to apologize to Mr. Donovan and all the Lawn Ornaments for putting so much pressure on them to win. I hope you'll all forgive me."

Mr. Gimpwater was nodding his head as fast as he could, but he would have agreed with Mr. Bumstock out of habit no matter what he said.

"Now I'm going to tell you why I've been such an old fool, and you're going to listen to me. The greatest thing that ever happened to me was playing on the Class D state championship team when I was at

Spruce Island High. It's true I've made a fortune in the lawn ornament business, but I've just been carrying on what my father started. Any idiot could have done it. But that championship, that was something I achieved without my father's help, and I'm still proud of it."

It was hard to picture Mr. Bumstock as a kid with a father.

He went on. "I've been sinking my money into our basketball team all my life, trying to get back the feeling I got playing on that team, but I never could do it."

Everybody was listening. Rodney ignored some hamburgers that were starting to burn.

"Just now when I was outside watching all of you enjoy yourselves in here, young Dewlap came out and invited me in. And *that's* when I got the old feeling back, the feeling I had when I played on that team for ol' Doc Thompson. It didn't have anything to do with winning ball games. It was a feeling of fitting in with people, of belonging. I'm going to tell you something for free: I haven't felt this good in sixty years—and I owe it all to Picasso Dewlap."

I felt pretty good, too.

Epilogue

———————●———————

I've written this epilogue to tell you what happened after we won the championship.

Mr. Bumstock offered Victor a partnership in the Bumstock Lawn Ornament Company, and he took it. Now they make traditional *and* avant-garde ceramic lawn ornaments. Some of Victor's nonrepresentational creations are selling pretty well, but the Ed statues are the most popular lawn ornaments of all, especially here in Maine.

The company used some of the money it made on advance orders for Ed statues to pay for the construction of a cabin for Ed and his parents in the north woods. Isn't that nice? Now he'll always be warm.

I see Ed about once a month. It's fun to go way up north to his place in Sasquatch country, but it's even more fun when he comes down to visit with me here on Spruce Island, the place where I fit in.